Dear Cerys

Tales From The Enchanted Forest

Brownie Pack Holiday

By

P. C. Crussell

much love

Grandpa and Grandma

Belief is a powerful gift

P. C. Crussell

5 xx

As always, to my wife, Jane, and my children, James and Lydia, for all your help with proof reading, and for your support and encouragement in writing this book.

The illustrations in this book have not been coloured in. This is so you can colour them in yourself.

Table of Contents

Tales From The Enchanted Forest

Chapter One

Getting Ready For Camp

For one weekend every summer the local Brownie pack would visit the local guiding centre and camp in the specially designed woodlands for the annual Brownie pack holiday.

It would start on Saturday, just after lunch, and finish on Sunday afternoon. The girls would play lots of super games, and over the weekend several Brownie badges could be earned. On Saturday evening the weekend highlight was having supper around the camp fire and singing traditional Brownie songs followed by the twilight trail. They would arrive back at the camp just before it got dark and drink a nice mug of hot chocolate, before snuggling into their sleeping bags and talking late into the night until they were too tired to stay awake any longer, or until the batteries in their torches ran down and there was no more light in the tents.

The twilight trail always took them through the wood surrounding the campsite; right around the site and as far as the wall nearest to where their tents were pitched. The girls would set off just before dusk which is the time that many animals like rabbits, mice and badgers would be waking up and leaving their nests for the night. This would also be the time when owls would be flying through the woods in their hunt for food. The best time, in fact, to see lots of woodland creatures.

Becca and Emma had joined the village Brownie pack the previous autumn and were both very excited to be going on this year's Pack Holiday.

On Friday Mummy had made sure Becca's Brownie uniform was clean, and had packed her a change of clothes in case she got dirty or it rained; although it hadn't rained properly for several weeks now and according to the weather forecast on television it didn't look like that was about to change. The country was in the grip of a drought and a heat wave that was, according to all the newspapers, breaking all previous records, but Mummy always prepared for every type of weather possible, so extra clothes and even a pac-a-mac were all in Becca's case.

"Where are you going?" asked Lily as Becca carefully folded her pyjamas and then threw them into her case where they quickly unfolded themselves again.

"We're going on a Brownie Pack holiday," she replied.

"Becca and I are Brownies," explained Emma, who always felt she had to explain everything, "and every year our Brownie Pack goes off for a weekend to the Guiding Centre to sleep in a tent for the night."

Cornflower laughed, "You're not Brownies," she said through her high-pitched giggles.

"But we are," said Becca. "Look, I've got the uniform and everything."

"What she means," said Lily, pushing her sister off the bed, "is that you don't look like any Brownies we know."

"Where we come from," Cornflower continued, flying back onto the bed and sitting on Lily, "Brownies are tiny and they are very hard working."

"And they expect a gift in return for their work," added Lily, huffing and puffing as she pushed Cornflower off her lap, "Get off me, Cornflower!"

"You started it," said Cornflower.

"I didn't," Lily replied.

"You did," Cornflower said, "you pushed me off the bed."

"Well..."

"Are there really such things as Brownies?" asked Becca, interrupting the arguing fairies. She was surprised, neither she nor Emma had ever heard of Brownies before except as Guides for little girls or the small chocolate cakes that Emma's Mummy sometimes made for them.

"Oh yes," the two Fairies replied together and giggled.

"What sort of gifts do they get given," asked Emma.

"Oh, lots of nice things; like berries and nuts," said Lily.

"Is that all?" asked Becca.

"Well sometimes they might get some pretty flowers, like daisies and dandelions, or an acorn cup of nice fresh spring water," Cornflower told them, "but they mostly prefer the berries and nuts."

"Don't they get any toys or anything?" asked Becca.

"Brownies don't need toys," Lily replied, "they only like to work hard, and if someone gives them gifts of food or drink then they'll work hard for them."

"And is that all the payment they want?"

Lily and Cornflower leapt into the air, flapping about and covering their ears with their hands.

"No! No, no, no!" Lily shouted in her high pitched little voice.

"What's wrong?" asked Emma, worried at the strange and sudden reaction.

"Brownies never, ever, get paid for the work."

"I don't understand," said Emma, "you just said..."

"We said that they expect a gift. If you give a gift to a Brownie then she'll do all the work you ever want," said Lily

"But if you call it payment," Cornflower continued, "then she'll leave you. Brownies don't like payment."

"But what's the difference?" Emma asked.

"Obligation," said Cornflower.

"Obli-what?" asked Becca.

"Obligation," Cornflower repeated.

"What does that mean?"

"Well, if you give a gift to a Brownie it's just that; it's a gift. When you give someone a gift, you give it to them because you want to give it to them and it means you don't expect anything in return. If the Brownie then decides to do lots of work for you, she does it because she loves to do work. If I give a Brownie a payment it's because I expect her to do something in return, for instance work. That's an obligation and Brownies don't like obligation, and that's when they'll leave you."

"I think I understand," said Becca, looking a bit puzzled.

"Do you have to work hard as a Brownie?" asked Cornflower brightly.

"Well," said Becca, "we have tasks to do and when we complete them we get given a badge to show we've done it."

"Just like real Brownies then," she replied. "You do a task and when you've done it you get a gift, which is your badge."

"I suppose so," Becca replied.

"So how many badges have you been given?"

"None yet," both girls replied together.

"We've really tried though," said Becca.

"We've just not managed to finish anything yet," Emma added.

"But we will do soon," Becca continued, "as soon as the new term starts after summer we are going to get some badges. Aren't we Em'?"

"Yes, we've nearly finished our nature observation badge, and if we see some more animals this weekend on the nature trail then we should get it. The first part was bird watching in the garden, that's when we found the Dove with the broken wing, do you remember?"

The Fairies nodded.

"And," Becca continued, "we are going to bake a cake on Mummy's birthday for our cookery badge."

"Oooh, can we help you?" Cornflower said with glee, flying into the air above the bed and clapping her hands together excitedly, "we love baking cakes, don't we Lily."

"Yes, baking cakes is one of our favourite things to do." Lily replied, and did a summersault over Becca's pillow.

"You could bake Fairy Cakes," Becca said with a giggle.

 "We can," said Cornflower, "yes, yes, yes. We're really good at baking Fairy Cakes."

"Or Chocolate Brownies," added Emma, and they all laughed together.

"We can make all sorts of things," said Lily, with an excited smile on her face.

"Oh," said Emma, shaking her head sadly and looking down to her feet.

"What's wrong?" Asked Becca.

"We have to bake the cakes on our own," she said, "not even Mummy is allowed to help us."

"But no one will know," insisted Lily, "and you don't have to tell anyone."

"No," said Becca, "but we'll know and it won't be right then. We want to earn the badge for something we've done on our own, then we'll feel proud that we've really earned it."

"OK," said Lily, barely able to disguise the disappointment in her little voice, "we'll just watch then." And with that she and Cornflower flew into the air and towards the open window. They turned to the girls as they were leaving, "see you later," they said and, with a wave of their tiny hands, they were gone.

"Crumbs," said Emma, looking sadly at where the Fairies weren't with a worried look on her face, "do you think we've upset them, Becca?"

"I don't know Em'," she replied quietly, "I do hope not."

But there was no time to think about it anymore because Mummy was calling up, telling them to get their things as it was time to go and Emma had to run off next door to collect her overnight bag.

Chapter Two

Pick Up Sticks and Brownie Points

The Florence Walker Guiding Centre was specially built for the local Guides, Brownies, Scouts and Cubs to use for their annual camps. It was set in eighteen acres, which is lots of space, of beautiful woodlands just a few miles drive from the village of Little Hamden, where they lived. It was surrounded by high brick walls with iron gates at the entrance, which made it safe and secure for the girls to camp there, but with loads of different activity options. There were four spacious clearings that were designated as campsites, with a concreted area for camp fires, and an area with brick built barbeques and ovens for cooking which meant that more than one Brownie or Guide pack could use the centre at the same time, and there was a pavilion near the entrance by the car park that had six dormitories, plus bathrooms, kitchens and an activity area so the centre could be used in winter as well as in summer.

Tents were set up at the end of each clearing away from the campfire. The rest of the clearing would be used for various games and activities over the weekend.

When Mummy dropped Becca and Emma off at the campsite, which was only a ten minute drive from the village, Mrs Morgan, who was Brown Owl, told them, to their delight, that they were sharing a tent with their school friends, Amy and Lydia. Neither of the girls had seen Amy or Lydia since the start of the long summer holiday, which now seemed ages and ages ago but was actually only four weeks, and the week after next, they would be going back to school again. How quickly the summer holidays had passed. Already both Becca's and Emma's Mummies had been buying school uniform in the sales.

"Put your things in your tent," said Brown Owl, "then go over there to Tawny Owl who is organising the gathering of wood and kindling for tonight's campfire."

"Enjoy yourselves you two," said Mummy, and she leant forward and kissed Becca, "Brownie Pack Holiday is always great fun."

The girls said goodbye to Mummy, who reminded them that Emma's Mummy would pick them both up tomorrow afternoon, and they watched her walk back to her car along the woodland path until she turned a corner and was gone.

The weeks of summer so far had been ever so hot and today was no different. The air in the clearing was still and the girls could feel the heat draining their energy, so that, despite their excitement at being on the pack holiday, all they really wanted to do was crawl into the shade of their tent and fall asleep. There was barely a sound to be heard in the forest. It was as though all the animals and birds had found themselves a nice bit of shade to rest for a while until the sun went down and the air in the woods had cooled enough for them to want to move again.

Across the clearing, almost lost in the shimmering heat, the girls could see Tawny Owl organising other girls and sending them off into the woods.

The two girls threw their rucksacks into their tent and dragged themselves across the clearing to join Tawny Owl and the other Brownies.

"Hey, you two," Amy called at the top of her voice, running over to greet them as they joined the other girls. With a noisy scream of joy, they hugged Amy and Lydia and immediately began chattering about what they had been doing during the summer holidays.

"Come on you four," said Tawny Owl, smiling at the four girls, "a little less chatter and a few more sticks and twigs please."

"Yes, Tawny Owl," they said and, on Tawny Owl's instruction, they ran off into the woods, with renewed energy, and started searching through the undergrowth for sticks and twigs.

* * * * *

"Hello."

"Oh, you made me jump," said Becca as she brushed some leaves away and Lily jumped out from under them.

"Surprise!"

She heard a little squeal and turned to see Cornflower bursting out of the undergrowth and flying around Emma.

"We've decided to come to enjoy the Brownie Pack Holiday too," said Lily, flying over to Cornflower. "Isn't it hot?" she added.

"Yes," said Becca, overjoyed to see the two little fairies again

"What do you want us to do?" asked Cornflower.

"Well," said Emma, "we've got to find and collect wood for the campfire first."

"Done," said Lily, clapping her hands together in glee.

"What do you mean 'done'?" asked Emma.

"We mean we've already built a pile of sticks and twigs, all you have to do is go and fetch them."

"Really?"

"Oh yes. Come on and follow us," said Lily, and she and Cornflower flew a bit further into the woods. There, behind a tree, was a pile of sticks, twigs and small branches that were ideal for a camp fire.

"Did you collect those sticks already?" asked Becca.

"Yes," Lily replied.

"But how did you know we needed them?"

"We heard that lady you called Tawny Owl tell you to collect sticks," said Cornflower.

"But that was only just now, just before we came into the woods," said Emma, "how did you manage to do that so quickly?"

"Magic," said Cornflower. "We're Fairies remember, we can do things like that."

So, gathering as much in their arms as they could carry, Becca and Emma returned to the field to show Tawny Owl how much they had collected.

"Oh well done, girls," she cooed as they emerged from the trees into the clearing, "what a splendid collection you've made, and so quickly too. Now," she continued, "put them all over there on that pile and run and see if you can find some more."

They dropped their collection of sticks onto the pile that was gathering there, and ran back into the woods to grab another armful from the stack of sticks that Lily and Cornflower had collected for them and returned to the clearing.

"Already?" said Tawny Owl as they emerged for a second time, "have you two just cut down your own tree?"

"No Tawny Owl," Becca replied, "we just got lucky."

"Well, at this rate you are going to win lots of tent points."

"Tent points?" said Emma, "what're they?"

"At the end of each task or game," Tawny Owl explained, "you will be awarded points for your tent and the tent with the most points at the end of the weekend, will get a special prize."

"We're going to win that prize," said Becca to Emma as they rushed back into the woods for more sticks and twigs.

"Let's get Amy and Lydia to help us with that pile," Emma suggested, "that way we can get maximum points," and so they called on their friends to follow them.

"Wow!" said Lydia "Wow! How did you find this?"

"We were lucky, I suppose," replied Becca, who noticed that the pile had got bigger since they had carried their last load.

"Maybe the forest Fairies left them for us," said Emma, gathering a huge armful and turning away to cover the smirk on her face as she tried to stop herself giggling. She and Becca could hear the giggles of Lily and Cornflower, which sounded like tiny bells tinkling in the undergrowth.

"Aw, wouldn't it be cool if it really was a Fairy pile," said Amy excitedly.

"But wouldn't they be cross with us?" asked Lydia.

"Why would they be cross with us?" asked Becca.

"Because we've just stolen from their wood pile," Lydia replied.

"Perhaps," said Emma, "they just put it there for us in the first place."

"Do you think so?"

"Yes, of course," said Emma, "why not?" And she picked up an armful of sticks and started off, "now come on, we want to win the tent points."

The other three followed Emma's example and followed her out of the woods and back to the clearing.

"What a wonderful job you girls are doing," said Tawny Owl as the four girls threw their sticks on the pile, "at this rate you'll get all the points for your tent."

"Wow," said Lydia, who always said 'wow' to everything, as they approached the pile of wood, "like wowie, wow. Look at this, someone's added more sticks to the pile while we've been gone. I'm sure there were never that many when we left last time."

"See what I said," said Emma with a laugh, "the Forest Fairies are looking after us today." And again, she could hear the giggles of Lily and Cornflower, this time coming from behind the tree.

As Amy and Lydia set off with another armful the two Fairies flew around to Becca and Emma, with big smiles on their tiny faces.

"See," said Lily, "we can help you."

"Yes," said Becca, "and we love you to help us, you are our friends."

"Are we?" asked Cornflower, squealing with delight, "are we really your friends?"

"Oh, yes," said Becca and Emma together.

"We love you," Emma continued, "you're so beautiful and you're so much fun."

Lily and Cornflower giggled with joy.

"She said we're beautiful," said Lily, flying around the little glade and clapping her hands excitedly.

"She was talking about me," said Cornflower to her sister, "she said I was beautiful."

24

"But she meant me too though, didn't she?" said Lily, looking worried.

"Of course not," replied her sister, "she just meant me. I've always been the pretty one."

Lily looked so sad that Emma thought she was going to cry.

"Of course I meant you too, Lily," she said and Cornflower burst out laughing and flew to Lily.

"Got you, got you," she laughed and then flew off into the trees chased by Lily.

"They're so funny," said Emma, watching them disappear into the trees. They could hear the Fairies' squeals of delight as they chased each other through the branches above them and, as they peered into the shadows, they could see other Fairies flying around.

"Look," said Becca, "there's Sienna and Amber."

"And Rose," added Emma.

They watched Rose as she stopped and hovered in the air between the trees. She turned and, smiling from ear to ear, waved at the two girls. Becca and Emma waved back as they watched the Fairies, their Fairies, as they thought of them, fly off into the woods.

"Come on," said Becca, "let's get these sticks on the camp fire."

When they got back to the clearing and they had thrown their armful of sticks and twigs onto the fire, Tawny Owl clapped her hands in delight and then called all the girls to gather around her.

The girls quickly lined up in their sixes. Becca, Emma, Lydia and Amy were all in the 'Pixies' Six. Their Sixer, Freya and their Seconder, Beth, both of whom were two years above them at school, were sharing a tent with Shelley and Nadia, who were the Sixer and Seconder of the 'Sprites' Six.

There were four Sixes in their Brownie Pack; The Pixies, The Sprites, The Gnomes and The Elves, and they were all split up into six tents of four girls while the Pack Leaders each had their own tent.

"Right girls," said Tawny Owl enthusiastically, "well done for collecting the sticks and twigs for our camp fire tonight. I've been keeping count of how much you each brought and the winning tent is tent four..."

"That's us," whispered Becca, nudging Emma with excitement.

"...Becca, Emma, Amy and Lydia, who are awarded with one tent point," and Tawny Owl made a mark on a piece of paper on her clipboard, "and one point for the Pixies Six," and they watched as Tawny Owl made another mark on her paper.

"Well done girls for winning the first points of the weekend, let's hope all of you earn lots of points and we all have a wonderful weekend."

Chapter Three

Potato Challenge

"Now," Tawny Owl continued, "please listen while I tell you about the activities for the weekend," and she started by telling the girls about how they were expected to be on their best behaviour for the whole of the weekend and any girls who had to be told off for anything during the weekend could lose a tent point and a point for their Six.

"We have a lovely weekend ahead of us," Tawny Owl continued, "first of all, we have some tasks to do to help prepare for this evening's dinner. Each tent will be given something to prepare and, once the task is done, there will be the nature scavenger hunt, which you will do in your Sixes, while Brown Owl and Snowy Owl prepare the meal.

"After dinner we shall light the campfire and we will sing some camp songs and after that I will lead the twilight trail before bed time.

"Breakfast tomorrow morning will be at eight o'clock, after which, we'll have a tent inspection and then we'll be clearing the tents and making sure that no litter is left, in fact, we must leave it so clean that people will wonder if we were ever here at all. After that, we've got a special surprise lined up for you, but we won't tell you what it is until the morning." There was a groan from the girls, they loved a surprise but they so wanted to know what the surprise was going to be.

"After that your Mummies and Daddies will be picking you up to take you home in time for lunch."

There was a general hubbub of noise as the girls all started talking at once, discussing the activities they were going to do and whether they'd be able to earn any badges. Tawny Owl clapped her hands together and called "Girls!" loudly.

Instantly the girls all fell silent and Tawny Owl read out the list of tasks for each of the Sixes and which Pack leader would supervise them. The Pixies task was peeling potatoes and they were going to be supervised by Snowy Owl, who was always ever so nice.

As Tawny Owl set them their tasks they heard Snowy Owl calling them and the Pixies' ran over to her.

"I don't know how to peel a potato," Becca told Emma as they ran across the camp site to start their task, "Mummy always does that sort of thing."

"I don't think any of us know," Emma replied, "my Mummy always has potatoes in the freezer, all sorts of them; chips, roasties, mash. I do hope Snowy Owl will show us how to do it."

"We can peel potatoes," said Cornflower, suddenly appearing from Emma's trouser pocket.

"Oh, yes," said Lily, landing on Becca's shoulder, "we're very good at peeling potatoes."

"Wow," said Becca, "how do you know how to peel potatoes?"

"Oh, we don't," Lily said with a smile, "we've never done it before."

"But," continued Cornflower, "we will be ever so good at it."

"Of course we will," said Lily as the two Fairies flew alongside Becca and Emma as they hurried across to Snowy Owl, "we always are."

Snowy Owl told the girls of Pixie Six to sit in a semi-circle in front of her. The six girls all sat down, and Lily and Cornflower sat between Becca and Emma, which meant they couldn't be seen by any of the others.

"Now girls," Snowy Owl said when they had all settled down and were looking at her expectantly, "peeling a potato is very easy if you use one of these special knives called a Potato Peeler." Snowy Owl picked up a potato and showed the girls how to use the peeler to peel away the brown skin of the potato to reveal the glistening yellow-white flesh beneath it, which she then put into a large pot full of cold water.

"Your turn," said Snowy Owl with a smile, and the girls each selected a potato and a peeler and started their work.

Becca held her peeler and scraped it carefully over the potato in her other hand. To her dismay nothing happened. The peeler had not cut into the skin of her potato at all so she tried again, pushing down harder this time. Again, she failed to make any cut in her potato. She looked over to Emma and saw that, although she was struggling to hold both the potato and the peeler, she had managed to peel some of the skin off her potato. She looked around and saw all the other girls were managing to work their peelers but, try as she might, she couldn't get hers to work.

She felt stupid and could feel tears welling up in her eyes. She couldn't understand why all the others seemed to be able to peel their potatoes and she couldn't.

She was suddenly aware of Snowy Owl standing in front of her and she looked up.

"I'm so rubbish," she said, sadly, holding up her peeler and her unpeeled potato to Snowy Owl, "I can't seem to do it."

"Oh, Rebecca dear, do not worry yourself so," said Snowy Owl kindly, "and never think you're rubbish, you're a clever girl. Now, I can see exactly what the problem is. You're left handed and these peelers are for right handed people. Here, try this one," and Snowy Owl passed Becca another peeler. "It's a left-handed peeler," she said, and to Becca's delight it worked and she was now able to peel her potato. Even so, it was still much more difficult than it had looked when Snowy Owl had shown them and, to help the girls she showed them all again.

Becca tried again and after a few minutes had only a small pile of peel in front of her and a half-peeled potato in her hand.

It really was quite difficult.

"We can do it quicker than you," whispered Lily in Becca's ear.

"You probably can," replied Becca glumly, as she and Emma both fumbled with their potatoes, "I'm not very good at it at all."

"Now we know what you need to do," said Cornflower, "it's quite easy. Watch." And the girls watched as the rest of the skin of the potatoes in their hands fell away, leaving them each with a perfectly peeled potato.

"Crikey," said Emma, "Brilliant."

"Brilliant," Becca agreed, then she said, "can you do them all?"

"Of course we can," said Lily, "we're Fairies, we can use Fairy magic." And without another word Lily and Cornflower flew to over the large pot, doing a strange little dance, up and down over the potatoes.

Then, with a little flutter of their wings and with a tiny splash as they touched the surface of the water, Lily and Cornflower dived right into the saucepan and, darting through the water like tiny little fish, and at such a speed that only Becca and Emma could see them, they watched the peel fall away from each potato.

Watching closely, it seemed to the two girls that Lily and Cornflower touched each potato in the pot in turn, but more than that, it seemed as though they were throwing something over them.

It was fascinating, magical, and they looked at each other excitedly.

After what seemed like ages, but really it was only a few seconds, the Fairies flew up and out of the saucepan, gasping for air as their heads broke the surface of the water, and flew back to the girls.

"All done!" said Lily, with a big smile on her face.

"We told you it was easy," said Cornflower as she sat in Emma's lap and shook all the water from her, splashing tiny drops into Emma's face.

"Golly!" whispered Emma, "how did you do that so fast?"

"And what," asked Becca, "were you throwing over those potatoes?"

"Fairy Dust, of course," said Lily, "what else?"

"All of our magic is made easier using Fairy Dust," explained Cornflower.

"Now," Cornflower continued, flying into the air and into the trees followed by her sister, "pretend you did it."

And that's exactly what they did.

One at a time, Becca and Emma picked peeled potatoes from their bucket and dropped them into the clean water.

The other girls, who had been concentrating hard on their task, hadn't seen what had happened and looked up in surprise and Becca and Emma dropped the last handful of potatoes into the saucepan and said loudly, "Finished."

"Golly," said Freya, looking into the saucepan with an amazed look on her face.

"Oh wow! Wowee," exclaimed Lydia, then added, "how did you manage to peel them so quickly?"

"Oh, well done," said Beth, "you managed that ever so quickly. You are clever."

"Oh well," said Becca, blushing slightly as she was being given credit for something that she hadn't actually done, "you know...?" and that was all she could say and the other girls just nodded and smiled at Becca and Emma with a look that suggested they did indeed know. Which they didn't ... really.

Snowy Owl was astonished.

"Well done girls," she exclaimed loudly, clapping her hands together in delight, "Pixies Six win over here, one Six point awarded to the Pixies for such a splendid job."

Becca and Emma thought they were going to burst as the other Sixes congratulated the Pixie Six by clapping, while the other girls in their Six patted them on the back.

As they waited for the other Sixes to complete their tasks they lay back on the grassy bank on the edge of the clearing, listening to the woodland noises.

A light breeze rustling the leaves in the branches above them; the cooing of Doves and the cawing of crows in the distance. They watched bees hovering amongst the wild flowers which grew at the sides of the woodland paths and they followed the flight of a butterfly as it flew beneath the trees, the colour of its wings bright in the rays of golden sunlight shining down from above.

Of all the beautiful sights around them, only Becca and Emma could see the several Fairies flying between the trees, some playfully chasing each other, while others were helping the bees in their search for pollen and they saw Rose fly across some wild pansy buds and, as she touched each one, they watched them open in a beautiful array of purple and white.

They gasped in wonder at the carpet of pretty flowers and Rose waved to them as she flew from flower to flower.

"Too busy to stop," she called to them, slightly out of breath, as she flew across the clearing and, as Rose flew over them, they saw hundreds of flowers burst open.

"It's what she does," said Lily, flying back to the girls.

"She's a Flower Fairy," added Cornflower, "her job is to make the flowers bloom when they should do, wake them up in the morning and put them to bed at night."

"Those flowers are what you call Wild Pansies," said Lily.

"We call them 'Love-In-Idleness'," Cornflower informed them, "it used to be a white flower, but silly Cupid shot it by mistake with one of his arrows and turned it purple."

"And because Cupid's arrow is the arrow of love, the flower can now be used as a love potion."

"Oh, that's so lovely," said Becca.

"When will the scavenger hunt start?" said Cornflower suddenly, "we love scavenger hunts, don't we Lily?"

"Oh yes," said Lily, and the girls could hear the excitement in her voice, "we're ever so good a scavenger hunts."

"Like you were ever so good at 'hide and seek'," said Becca, with a smile, "when you gave yourselves away because you couldn't stop giggling?"

"That was her fault," said Lily, "she's a terrible giggler."

"And so are you," replied Cornflower, starting to giggle once more, "you usually start it."

"I don't. I usually giggle because you giggle."

"I think...," said Emma.

"Yes?" said Lily and Cornflower together.

"I think," said Emma, "that you are both as bad as each other."

And she was probably right.

Chapter Four

The Nature Scavenger Hunt

The grassy bank was warm and the soft, gentle buzzing of the bees as they flew from flower to flower in the long grasses made the girls drowsy. It was such a lovely afternoon and the Pixie Six, having finished their own task so quickly, had to wait while the Sprites; the Gnomes and the Elves Sixes all finished theirs.

The Sprites had had to shell peas, the Gnomes had had to 'top and tail' runner beans and the Elves had had carrots to scrape. The Pixies had probably had the most difficult of the tasks to complete but, thanks to Lily and Cornflower and their Fairy Magic, they had finished first and had earned a Six point as a result.

A strange buzzing noise disturbed the peaceful afternoon and the girls looked around to see where it was coming from. Freya had fallen asleep and the buzzing noise was the sound of her snoring. The girls all nudged each other and sniggered, then Beth pointed to the top of the mound, indicating that she wanted them all to move up the bank without disturbing Freya.

As quietly as they could they all stood up and crept further up the bank, leaving Freya lying peacefully on her back, still snoring.

"Now," whispered Beth, "let's throw something at her to wake her up and see what happens." And with that she picked up a small handful of moss from the ground and threw it in Freya's direction. It was a terrible throw and the moss landed several feet away from Freya, with no chance of disturbing her at all.

"Lily," whispered Becca.

"You're playing a prank on your friend," said Lily, "and you want us to help? Are you allowed to play pranks on your friends?"

"Oh, it's only a bit of fun," explained Emma, "we won't do anything to hurt her, will we Becca?"

"We won't be nasty," Becca confirmed, "we're just having some fun."

"Won't she be cross?" asked Cornflower.

"Golly, I hope not," Becca replied, "we don't want to upset her."

"We can fly over and tickle her if you like," said Lily, "would that be fun?"

"Oh yes, ever so," both girls replied and they watched the two little Fairies fly over to where Freya was lying.

"Oh, look at those two Dragonflies," said Beth, pointing down the mound, "they look as though they are going to land on Freya."

From a distance the two little Fairies did, indeed, look like they were Dragonflies, especially to eyes that had never seen real Fairies before and the girls watched in astonishment as Cornflower perched lightly on Freya's nose and started to dance on it. In her sleep, Freya waved her hand in front of her face to move whatever it was that was tickling her nose as Lily, standing on the ground by Freya's head, pulled up a blade of grass and gently poked it in Freya's ear.

Shaking her head and waving her hands in the air Freya sat up suddenly as Lily and Cornflower flew away and into the woods, returning, unseen, to Becca's and Emma's sides a few seconds later.

Freya sat there for a few moments, looking around and blinking, as though she was trying to remember where she was but on hearing the laughing behind her turned and saw the rest of her Six team.

"Was that you lot?" she asked, getting up and walking towards them.

"Oh, my goodness, Freya," said Beth, still giggling, "you fell asleep and these two Dragonflies, literally, just, like, landed on you. It was so funny."

* * * * *

"Right girls," said Tawny Owl, clapping her hands together and walking across the campsite with a handful of cloth tote bags, "gather around me now, it's time for the nature scavenger hunt."

All the girls cheered "Hooray!" and they ran across to where Tawny Owl was standing in the middle of the field.

"You've all been wonderful girls and completed your task, and I must say, you've done better than we've seen for many year, well done everyone. Now," she continued, handing each Sixer a tote bag which contained and sheet of paper with a list of tasks and a pencil with a clean, white rubber on one end, "I want you to read the list of things to find very carefully before you set off. When you are ready and know what you are going to do then you can set off, in your own time, and you can go anywhere in the site, so there's no need to follow each other. We'll all meet back here in one hour."

They all went to different corners of the field, together in their Sixes, and read carefully through the list. The Nature Scavenger Hunt listed fifteen objects for the girls to find in the woods of the Guiding Centre.

Nature Scavenger Hunt

Your task is to find the following items and bring them back to base in the tote bag provided (Please do not disturb nests, sets, or any wildlife in the woods)

Two kinds of seeds
Two different types of leaves
A Beautiful stone
An Acorn
An egg shell
A pinecone
A chewed leaf

A snail shell
A stick
A feather
Something straight
Something round
Something smooth
Something rough
Something green

Freya, as the Pixies' Sixer, took charge of the tote bag and its contents. "Right," she said, "I think the best way to win this is to divide us all into three pairs and I will allocate five objects for each pair to find. Once each pair has found their own five then they are to help another pair who hasn't found all theirs yet.

"Becca, you go with Emma and make the first pair," Becca and Emma smiled at each other, "Lydia, and Amy will make the next pair and I'll make the third pair with Beth."

They all lay on their tummies on the warm grass facing each other in a circle as Freya told each pair the objects they had to find.

"Now, when we go off," she told the other five, "we'll stay together but you just look for the things you have been told to collect until you've got all yours, right?"

"Right Freya," they all replied.

"OK. Now Becca and Emma, you will look for the first five items on the list; from two kinds of seeds to an acorn, including everything in between," - "Easy

peasy," whispered Lily in Becca's left ear, - "Lydia and Amy, you'll take the next five, so from a pinecone to a feather, and me and Beth will have the last five items, all the 'somethings', from something straight to something green.

"Right Pixies," Freya shouted out loud, to show the other Sixes that they were ready and knew what they were doing, "let's go out there and win."

All the girls of Pixie Six let out a cheer as they jumped up and set off into the woods surrounding the campsite. They followed their leader out of the clearing and along one of the woodland paths leading from their campsite.

The surrounding woods were quiet. There was very little breeze to rustle the leaves in the branches above them and they could smell the sweet scent of the hundreds of tiny flowers that covered the woodland floor. The Bluebells, being spring flowers, had now lost their petals but Dog Rose, with their beautiful pink flowers, purple Foxglove and Wild Pansies, spread out on either side of the path in a carpet of colour. In patches where the sunlight shone down through the canopy of branches above them, large bunches of ferns had taken root and in an instance Freya hopped into the woods and pulled off one of the leaves. She turned to the others with a big smile.

"Something green," she said, waving the fern leaf at them, "only another four things to get," and she placed the fern in the tote bag.

"We'd better start looking for our stuff," said Becca, leaving the path and picking her way through the ferns and woodland flowers, followed by Emma as they set about their hunt.

They were concentrating hard on searching the forest floor for things when a loud rumpus above them made them jump in fright. They had disturbed two large wood pigeons and, as they flapped loudly in the branches to get away from them, a number of leaves fluttered down to the woodland floor. Emma caught one.

"That's one type of leaf," she said to Becca, "let's find another before we look for the other things."

A squeal of delight from Lydia and Amy announced that they, too, were having some success with their finds.

"That's an Ash leaf," Cornflower told them, you can tell by the way it's made up of lots of little leaves, "I can get a Sycamore leaf to go with it," and with that she flew up into the trees.

Seconds later they watched as Cornflower floated down towards them holding onto a stalk of a leaf as though she was holding onto a parachute. She gently glided down and landed on Emma's hand.

"There you are," she said, "one leaf, different from the other."

"Ooh," said Emma, "that looked so much fun. I wish I could do that."

"You're far too big to be able to float on a Sycamore leaf," said Lily, dancing in the air in front of them, "so you'll just have to get on with your next task." And she flew up into the same tree that her sister had just been in. They watched her pull something off a branch, something that looked like a pair of Fairy wings, and, as she flew back over the two girls, she let it go. They watched it, fascinated, as it twirled through the air, spinning down towards them. As they ran beneath it, with their hands open wide to try and catch it, it seemed to change direction.

"What is it?" asked Becca as she snatched it out of the air and looked at it, laying there in her hand. Even close up it seemed to be a pair of wings.

"It's a Sycamore seed, of course," said Lily, landing on her shoulder. "Actually, it's two seeds joined together to make a pair of wings. When they fall off the tree they spin round like helicopter wings."

"Actually," said Cornflower, "it spins like that to make it land as far away from the tree as it can get. If it's windy it can get blown miles away to somewhere else."

49

"So that's one of our seeds then," said Becca, pleased, "let's take all this and put it in the bag and we can go and find the rest then." They picked their way back through the thick undergrowth to where Freya and Beth were searching. Freya had hung the tote bag on a stubby branch of a nearby tree.

"Well done you two," said Beth and she saw them put their finds in the bag. "Still loads of things to find yet though."

Becca and Emma turned to continue their search.

"Oh look," said Becca as they crossed the path and moved back into the little clearing where they had been searching, "a Fairy Clock." She stooped down to pull up a thick green stalk on top of which was a large fluffy white head.

"Why do you call it a Fairy Clock?" asked Lily.

"Because you're meant to blow on it...." Becca started to say.

"And when you blow on it," Emma, who always explained everything, explained, "the white fluffy bits fly away. When they fly people think they look like Fairies and the amount of puffs it takes to blow all the fluffy bits off is meant to tell you what time it is in Fairyland."

"But they look nothing like Fairies," said Lily and flew in front of Emma, "see," she pointed to herself,

"I'm a Fairy and I look nothing like that," and she pointed to the white fluffy head of the Fairy Clock.

"It's actually a ball of Dandelion seeds," explained Cornflower, "so there's your second and different seed."

"Really?"

"Yes, those white fluffy things that you think are Fairies are seeds."

"And they look nothing like Fairies," added Lily, "us Fairies are pretty, and you humans are silly for thinking that we look like Dandelion seeds."

"We don't think you look like Dandelion seeds, or rather I don't think Dandelion seeds look like Fairies. I know what Fairies look like."

"But," added Emma, "most people aren't like us, most people have never seen a real Fairy so maybe they think they look like those seeds."

"Hahaha," giggled Cornflower, "that's even sillier. There's pictures of Fairies everywhere. I saw some pictures of Fairies in one of your books and they looked like real Fairies to me."

"Silly or not," said Becca, "We've got another of our things we have to collect." And she ran over to the bag and carefully dropped it in.

"Anyway," she said when she returned, "I prefer to call it a Fairy Clock than a Dandelion seed. Now where will we find an acorn?" she continued as she jumped over a small log hidden in a clump of Dog Rose.

"Under an Oak tree, of course," replied Lily. "Do you not know that?"

"Of course I know that," Becca snapped back, "I know acorns come from Oak trees. What I meant was where can we find an Oak tree?"

They stood amongst the trees and looked all around them. They could see Lydia and Amy in the small clearing on the other side of the path. They were crouching down over something they'd found on the ground. They jumped up and Lydia waved a long brown feather over her head and joyfully trotted over to Freya and Beth to drop it in the bag.

"We're having trouble finding a chewed leaf," Amy called over to Becca and Emma, "got any ideas?"

"You could pick any leaf and bite off a bit of it with your teeth," Becca called back

"You're so silly," Amy replied and they all laughed, "but we might have to do just that if we can't find a real one." She turned away and continued with her search.

The part of the woods in which they were searching had Ash, Sycamore and Beech trees, but there were no Oaks to be seen.

"I'll fly over the woods and find one," said Cornflower and she flew up through the branches and disappeared above the trees.

"While she's doing that," said Emma, "we might as well try and get the other two things we've got left. An egg shell and a beautiful stone."

"Stones are boring," said Becca, "they're just brown or grey. There's nothing beautiful about a stone."

"Let's try and find an egg shell first then, shall we?" her friend replied.

"Crikey, we do get the hard ones, don't we, Em? Where do we start?"

"If you want to find an egg shell," Lily said, flying around them both, "you need to look for a nest. If you find a nest you might find an egg shell beneath it."

So, they looked up.

They saw branches and leaves and sky and more branches and more leaves and ....

"There's one," said Becca suddenly, pointing up. Emma looked to where she was pointing and, sure enough, not too far above them, in the lowest branches of the tree they were under, was a large nest which had been carefully woven with twigs, grass and moss.

From where they stood the nest appeared to be empty and, although it was on the lowest branches it was still too far above them to reach and the branch it was on was too thin for them to climb on. So, they started to search the ground beneath it instead.

As they crawled about on their hands and knees, searching through the undergrowth of weeds, ivy vines and flowers, they heard their names being called in a high-pitched voice above them. They looked up and burst out laughing, all they could see was Lily's tiny face peering over the side of the nest and her hand, waving at them.

"Cooee!" she called down and a big smile broke out on her face as the girls looked up at her.

"What can you see?" Becca called up.

"You," Lily replied and waved again.

"No silly," Becca said, "I mean can you see any egg shells?"

"Oh yes," she replied, "loads. I'll bring one down."

"Can you bring the whole nest down?" asked Emma.

"Oh no," said Lily, as she flew down holding a bright blue egg shell. "No. No, I can't do that."

"Why not, is it too heavy?"

"No, it's not too heavy, I can lift things that are

much heavier than that. It's a Thrush's nest."

"Is it empty?"

"Oh yes, it's quite empty at the moment."

"Then why can't we have the whole nest? We could take it into school, it would make a lovely nature study," said Becca.

"Thrushes take weeks building their nests and they use it all through spring and summer. In a nice summer, they might lay three or four lots of eggs and this summer is still lovely."

"Do you think they'll lay some more eggs then?" asked Emma.

"Oh yes. I spoke to Mrs Thrush just now. She's going to lay some more eggs real soon. Here's your egg shell."

Lily handed the girls half an egg shell. It was quite empty and clean inside and the outside was a bright shiny blue in colour with dark brown spots all over it.

"Golly, isn't it beautiful," said Emma, looking at the tiny shell which was about the same size as the tip of her finger.

"Thank you, Lily," said Becca, "we'd better be really careful with this. It looks so fragile and we don't want to break it."

"When the Thrushes have finished with their nest I'll bring it to you," said Lily.

"Will you? Will you really?" asked Becca.

"Yes, the last lot of babies will be leaving the nest in a few weeks and then they'll have no more need for it. They usually build a new one next year."

Becca took out a tissue from her pocket and carefully wrapped the fragile egg shell up before running over to Freya and Beth to put it carefully in the tote bag.

"What's that?" asked Beth as she watched Becca put the tissue in the bag.

"It's an eggshell," said Becca, "we found an empty Thrush's nest and it had some eggshells in it."

"Oh, well done. What have you got left now?"

"An acorn and a beautiful stone," she replied, "but I don't know where we'll find a beautiful stone."

"Oh, I'm sure you'll find something amazing," said Beth, encouragingly, and she turned back to her own searching.

"I wonder where Cornflower has got to," said Emma as Becca ran back to her and Lily.

"I'm sure she'll be back soon," Becca replied, "maybe she's having difficulty finding an Oak tree."

"What do you think Lily?" asked Emma, turning to the busy little Fairy who was hovering over some bright yellow buttercups she had found in the clearing as she was looking for a beautiful stone.

Lily flew over to the girls, who had sat down in the warm sun, and landed on a little toadstool which was growing in the shade of the nearby ferns. She crossed her legs, put her hands on her forehead and closed her eyes.

The girls watched as Lily sat there, absolutely still and silent, clearly concentrating on something.

"What's she doing?" whispered Becca to Emma.

"Shh!" Emma replied, watching Lily.

Then Lily opened her eyes wide and sat bolt upright.

"She needs our help," she said, flying into the air, "come on."

"Is she in trouble?" asked Becca, concerned. She remembered the last time the sisters had gotten into trouble when they locked themselves in the fridge at home.

"Oh goodness, what's wrong?" asked Emma, also worried that Cornflower might be in some serious danger.

"Well, she's not in any danger," said Lily, putting their minds to rest, and she could see the looks of relief on the two girls' faces, "but she is stuck and needs our help."

"Can you tell where she is?"

"Follow me," said Lily, flying across the clearing towards the trees, "she's not very far away."

The girls jumped up and ran after Lily, into the woods and away from the path.

The branches of the trees above them were woven together to form a thick canopy, like a roof over their heads. The canopy effectively blocked out the sunlight and their eyes had to adjust to the gloomy shadows. It was also nice and cool in the shade of the woods and the girls could hear the rustling of small animals as they scurried about in the undergrowth.

Lily carefully flew beneath the trees, flying slowly to allow the girls to keep up with her. She seemed in no hurry.

Actually, as the girls got close to her they were surprised to hear her giggling to herself.

"What's so funny?" asked Emma.

"You'll see," said Lily, turning back to face them, "you'll see." And she flew on ahead again. "Come on, keep up you slow coaches."

"That's easy enough," replied Becca, who was panting now, partly from the running and partly from the heat, "you're not exactly flying fast," and, putting on a spurt of speed, she ran right past Lily.

"Whoa," said Lily as Emma also ran past her, "you nearly ran right into Cornflower."

They all stopped.

Becca and Emma looked around them. The trees in this part of the woods grew quite close to each other and all around them on the ground, were dense bunches of ferns that came up to their waists.

Lily landed on a nearby fern and rolled on her back laughing uncontrollably as she pointed to one of the trees. They looked but, at first, couldn't see anything.

"Cornflower?" said Emma, in a whisper.

"I''m over here," they heard the tiny voice of Cornflower reply and they looked to where they had heard her voice.

Then they saw her, hanging in front of them. She certainly wasn't flying because her wings weren't beating. She was just hanging, apparently in mid-air, with a brown acorn cup perched haphazardly on her head and a green acorn clutched in her hands. She hung there, quite still, about level with Becca's and Emma's head.

Lily was still laughing uncontrollably.

"Silly Cornflower," she gasped, trying to catch her breath. The children could see tiny blue tears of laugher rolling down her cheeks and Cornflower just grinned, sheepishly, not moving.

At first Becca and Emma couldn't understand why Cornflower was in mid-air without flying but, as they approached her, it all became clear.

"Oh goodness," Emma exclaimed, and the two girls stood there not knowing whether to laugh or be concerned.

Cornflower had flown into a spider's web and, as she was not flying very fast at the time, she hadn't been able to fly right through it. Its sticky threads had caught her, wrapped themselves around her and trapped her there. She was hanging nearly five feet above the ground.

The web had been woven between two nearby branches and it was still taught. Not concentrating at the time, Cornflower had flown right into it, her arms and legs had gone through the gaps in the web but her head and body had become caught by the strong silken strands, their strength had stopped her flying through and their stickiness had prevented her from flying backwards out of it.

"Do you like my new hat?" she said with a smile, pointing to the acorn cup on her head and Becca and Emma started laughing.

"We'll get you out," said Emma, but she made no move to help Cornflower because she was scared of spiders and was frightened that the spider might run out and crawl up her arm.

"Erm..." she said.

"I'll do it," said Becca, stepping forward. She knew all about her friend's fear of spiders.

"Careful," said Cornflower and Becca gently grasped her waist between her thumb and forefinger.

"Don't worry, I'll be as gentle as I can," said Becca.

"I meant," replied Cornflower, "that we must be careful not to do too much damage to the web, it takes a spider a lot of energy to weave one."

"Lucky for you the spider didn't mistake you for a fly and try to eat you," Becca said to Cornflower as she gently pulled her back. The silken strands of the web stretched and then slowly peeled away setting Cornflower free from her sticky prison.

"She did come out and check whether I was worth eating," Cornflower told them, "and she was quite disappointed when she discovered I wasn't a fly. Actually, she was a bit cross because she thought I was going to ruin her web and she'd have to build it again but I told her that when my friends arrived I'd make sure they were careful. She was alright then and we were chatting until you arrived."

"Really?"

"Oh, yes," Cornflower replied, "she was quite chatty. I think she gets a bit lonely because no-one much likes spiders and she likes to chat. She told me how much she was enjoying the summer. She said the warm weather had been good to her because lots of flies had hatched and flown into her web and her larder is full enough to keep her going all through winter."

"Ooh, yuck," said Emma, "that's gross."

"Where is she now then?" said Becca, who found spiders quite fascinating.

"She hid when you and Emma arrived. She's very shy."

"Shy?" Becca couldn't understand how a spider could possibly be shy.

"Yes. You humans are so big and clumsy. When you are running about you just run through spider webs and break them, so spiders are scared of you. Do you want to meet her? I can ask her to come out if you want."

"Oh yes, please," said Becca.

"No!" said Emma, "please don't. Spiders are so yucky."

"Come on you lot," said Lily, who had recovered from her fit of laughing, "we've still got one more item left to find for your nature scavenger hunt."

"Actually," said Cornflower to Emma as they turned and ran through the woods to get back to their clearing, "spiders are lovely creatures and they are much more frightened of you than you are of them."

"But they have all those legs and things, and they bite you."

As she was running through the woods and talking to Cornflower Emma didn't notice a root sticking up from the woodland floor. Her foot caught in it and she was suddenly flying through the air. She landed heavily on the ground with a thump which drove all the breath from her and she bounced across the woodland floor.

As she landed her knee struck something sharp with quite a force. She let out a cry as an excruciating pain shot through her and she rolled over on the ground. She sat up, screwed her face up with pain and grasped hold of her knee. There was a deep cut and already blood was dripping from the wound and pouring down her leg.

The pain was unbearable.

"Ow! Ow! Ow!," she wailed, tears already pouring down her cheeks.

"Em'," said Becca, running back to her friend, "Oh Em', are you alright?" She could see that Emma was clearly not alright, she was crying loudly and holding onto her knee which was bleeding heavily, and she knew it was a silly thing to say, but she couldn't think of anything else.

Becca knelt down next to Emma and held her protectively in a tight hug. She felt her t-shirt getting wet from Emma's tears and she held her even tighter, rocking her gently.

"Let us see," said Cornflower, gently pulling Emma's hand away from the deep gash on her knee.

Lily landed on Emma's leg alongside her sister and they both carefully inspected the wound.

"Ooh, nasty," said Cornflower, which made Emma cry even more, "but don't worry, nothing's broken so we can help."

With that, both Fairies lent forward and placed a small kiss on Emma's knee.

Immediately the pain was gone and Emma opened her eyes wide, still sobbing, but no longer hurting.

She watched in amazement as the two Fairies continued to place their healing kisses on her bleeding knee.

"Wow," whispered Becca, entranced by what she was seeing.

Eventually, as the wound slowly disappeared, Emma stopped sobbing, and soon there wasn't even a scratch to show that there had been a cut at all.

Becca handed Emma another tissue and she wiped the blood from her leg then, wiping the tears from her eyes with the back of her hand, blew her nose and got up.

"Oh wow," exclaimed Becca, "come and look at this."

Emma carefully started to walk forward and was pleased to find that there was no pain in her knee at all.

"What?" She looked down to where Becca was staring and there on the ground, where she had just been sitting, was a large stone which had broken into two when Emma's knee had struck it. The inside of the stone was made up from several different brightly coloured layers.

Becca picked it up and turned it over in her hands. "What a beautiful stone," she said.

It was like a tiny rainbow with a layer of yellow on top of which was a bright layer of red. Various brown and yellow layers surrounded them and there was even orange and a shiny black layer. They had never seen a stone quite as beautiful.

"Our beautiful stone," said Lily, clapping her hands together and flying around it, "isn't it pretty."

"We've found everything now," added Cornflower joyfully. There were still strands of spider web silk stuck to her dress and legs, and she still wore the acorn cup on her head as a funny little hat.

The two girls entered the clearing and marched over to the others. Becca dropped the acorn into the tote bag and the two girls proudly showed off the coloured rock they had found.

"See," said Beth, "I told you you'd come up with something amazing, didn't I?"

Becca just smiled and she felt herself blushing.

"Well, we've got everything on the list now," said Freya, picking up the, now full, tote bag they had been given, "so let's get back to camp and give these in."

Chapter Five

Super Supper and Faulty Fire

The campsite was buzzing with activity as the girls of Pixies Six returned to the field with their tote bag full of treasure. They were pleased with themselves, having managed to find everything that was on their list of things to find.

Freya's plan of dividing the list between the six of them so they worked in pairs had been a clever one, and had enabled them to complete the Nature Scavenger Hunt in good time, and ahead of the other Sixes.

As they entered the clearing they could see their Pack Leaders working hard.

An area of the clearing had been specially laid with

concrete so that the campers who visited the centre were able to light camp fires safely and without endangering the surrounding woodland. These areas, and there was one in each campsite, had been given the name "the fire pit". In the fire pit there was an area where the girls could build a bonfire, which they had done when they first arrived earlier in the day, and, in the corner of the fire pit was a large area with a brick built barbeque and a large stove where saucepans and cauldrons could be heated up, and this was where Brown Owl and Barn Owl were right now, cooking all the vegetables that the girls had prepared earlier. They were checking the cauldrons and saucepans which contained potatoes, carrots, runner-beans and peas. Every so often one of them would lift a lid and release a huge cloud of steam from one of the cauldrons.

Snowy Owl was working in a thick cloud of smoke and they could hear the loud sizzling as she cooked the burgers and sausages on the barbeque.

The smell of barbeque cooking wafted across the field making their mouths water and their tummies rumble as they realised how hungry they were.

Tawny Owl saw the girls of Pixies Six arriving back at the campsite and called them over to her. They ran down the dry, grassy bank and over to the tables at the other side of the clearing.

"That was quick, girls, did you find everything?"

"Oh, yes," said Freya, still panting, as they all were, from their run across the field.

"And how did you finish so quickly, did you just get lucky or did the Forest Fairies help you?" As she said this she winked at the girls and smiled to show that she was just joking, and took the tote-bag from Beth, who had carried it back to camp for them.

"I split the Six up into three teams of two and gave each team five things to find," said Freya, proudly.

"Oh, well done. That shows good leadership, Freya, I shall make sure Brown Owl knows how clever you've been. Now, let's see what you've got."

Tawny Owl carefully unpacked the bag, smoothed it out over the table and started to lay out all the pieces the girls had collected on top of it, ticking them off as she went. Freya explained that their 'something straight' was a short brown twig; there was a white stone that was perfectly flat on two sides and almost completely round, like a two pence coin, so it counted as their 'something round' and also as their 'something smooth' and their 'something rough' was a piece of bark that they'd found on the woodland floor beneath some ferns.

Tawny Owl laid out the rest of the find, carefully unwrapping the fragile egg shell from the tissue and, finally, she looked at the multi-coloured stone they had found.

"That is so beautiful," she said, as she picked it up and turned it over and over in her hand, watching how the sunlight caught the bright colours and made them sparkle. "What a lovely find, well done."

By now the girls from the other Sixes were arriving back at the camp. They ran over to where the

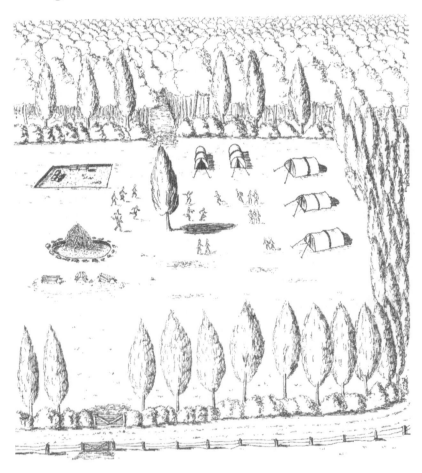

girls of Pixies Six were standing and each presented their tote-bags to Tawny Owl.

Tawny Owl unpacked all their finds, again laying out everything carefully on the tote-bags they had been collected in.

The Sprites Six and the Gnomes Six had both managed to find fourteen of the fifteen items on the list, and each earned a point for their Six; The Elves and The Pixies had both found all fifteen items and were each awarded two points for their Six.

"You've all done a wonderful job with the Scavenger Treasure Hunt," said Tawny Owl, when she had finished the sorting and checking, "did you all enjoy it?"

The enthusiastic cheers from the girls as they all bounced up and down around Tawny Owl confirmed that they had, indeed, all had a fabulous time and that they were clearly all still full of energy.

"Right girls," Tawny Owl continued once the girls had stopped bouncing about and were paying attention to her, "in a minute we'll be serving up dinner. As you can see Brown Owl, Snowy Owl and Barn Owl have been busy cooking all those lovely vegetables you prepared earlier to go with the burgers and sausages. We also have a number of veggie burgers and sausages for those of you who said you were vegetarians on your Pack Holiday application form."

Tawny Owl waited while the girls again jumped around in their excitement.

"After dinner," she continued eventually, "we will light the camp fire. The fire will be lit by the four Sixers, who will each light a part of the wood pile, and I will show you which part each of you will light. When we come to light it you will be given a firelighter taper and you'll light your bit of the fire only when I tell you to do so.

"I would remind you all that fire can be very dangerous if you do not follow the rules, and we do not want any accidents, do we?"

Tawny Owl looked at the girls, waiting for them to reply.

"No Tawny Owl," the girls said in unison.

"Exactly," Tawny Owl continued, "and if you all do as I say, and especially keep a safe distance from the fire then no one will come to any harm.

"Then, once the fire is lit, we'll all gather around it and sing some campfire songs with Barn Owl, who has brought her guitar with her. And later this evening, before it gets dark, you'll each go out with a Group Leader for the Twilight Nature Trail."

Another series of cheers interrupted her. The Twilight Nature Trail was always one of the highlights of the Brownie Pack Holiday weekend and, if the girls were lucky, they could see a real owl or two, some rabbits and some squirrels, and if they did, they would, most likely, gain their nature badge, provided they had spent some time at home doing their Garden Watch task, which Becca and Emma had.

"And remember, all of you, if you want to see as many animals as possible, you will all have to learn to be as silent as mice and not as noisy as the herd of elephants you sound like right now."

The girls laughed at being called a herd of elephants, and some of them crouched forward and waved their arm in front of their face pretending it was an elephant's trunk.

"Tawny Owl," Brown Owl called out from the fire pit, "we are nearly ready to serve up so can you make sure that the girls are ready?"

There was another loud burst of shouts and excited squeals from the girls to let Brown Owl know that the girls were not only ready, but also very hungry.

"If you could send the girls to the pavilion to go and wash their hands for dinner," Brown Owl continued, shouting over the noise, "then, when they are ready, please send them over in their Sixes and they can form an orderly queue."

"Girls," said Tawny Owl, "you all heard what Brown Owl said, so please go and wash your hands then you can line up in your sixes and I will tell you when you can go."

In less than five minutes the girls had lined up, as instructed, and were standing quietly. Tawny Owl

said, "Pixies Six, as you are currently ahead on points you girls can go first," and without stopping to hear anything more the girls of Pixies Six ran across the field to the fire pit where they lined up behind Freya and Beth, who then handed out paper plates and plastic knives and forks to Becca, Emma, Lydia and Amy.

It was a super feast. Burgers and sausages in a fresh white roll, with freshly cooked vegetables. There was tomato ketchup, brown sauce, mayonnaise and mustard for the burgers and sausages for anyone who wanted it, and even real butter to put on the potatoes.

And there was real home-made cloudy lemonade to drink. This was made by Barn Owl, who had once been on a cookery competition program on television and had come third.

With food piled high on their plates the girls quickly returned to the tables. Tawny Owl had now cleared away the treasure, and they sat down to eat.

All the girls were chattering excitedly, quick to talk about their afternoon adventures in the woods, and more than once Becca and Emma had to stop themselves talking about Lily and Cornflower.

The food was delicious and very soon there were twenty-four full up girls and twenty-four empty plates.

"Now, who wants some more cloudy lemonade," asked Barn Owl as she walked across to the table carrying two large jugs in her hands.

Without exception, every girl noisily jumped up with a shout of "yes please" and waved their cup in the air at Barn Owl for it to be refilled.

"Excuse me, Barn Owl," said Gemma, who was in the Sprites Six and in Becca's and Emma's class at school.

"Yes, Gemma," said Barn Owl, turning to the girls with a smile.

"How do you make your cloudy lemonade? It's ever so nice."

"Why, thank you Gemma," she replied, "I am glad you like it. It's quite a simple recipe really," she continued with a smile, "I use real lemons and real clouds."

"Real clouds?" Another girl called out. "Really?

"Oh, yes, but not just any old cloud, they have to be special ones," she told them. Her voice dropped to a whisper and she continued, as if she was going to share a special secret with them, "they must be clouds that have been touched by a rainbow after the rain on a sunny day."

All the girls looked up into the sky. There were just a few, tiny, fluffy white clouds floating in an otherwise clear blue sky and when they looked back at Barn Owl she was walking back across the field to the other pack leaders, leaving the girls with lots of questions.

"How does she get clouds?" one girl asked.

"She's fibbing, of course," said another, "she'd have to be able to fly if she put real clouds in it."

"Maybe she's a witch," another girl suggested, and they all looked serious for a moment, then someone said, "Yeah, and every time it rains she flies up on her broomstick and fills up jam jars with clouds," and they all started to giggle.

"Must be difficult catching a cloud," said Lydia, looking up to the sky with a dreamy look on her face, "I mean, they fly across the sky ever so quickly."

"I don't see why," said Shelley from Elves Six, "there's usually loads of them up there, and we usually get plenty of rain."

"But they have to be touched by a rainbow," Lydia replied, "that's what she said."

"That's probably why her lemonade tastes so nice," said Nadia, who was also in Elves Six and Shelley's best friend.

"Aeroplanes fly through clouds," said Emily, who was the Sprites Sixer. "Perhaps she knows someone who flies planes and who can get them for her every time he flies through them."

"Maybe she gets them from Amazon," said Shelley. "My mum is always ordering things from Amazon. My dad gets ever so cross with her."

"Maybe," said Amy, "she gets them from the Fairies.

"Oh, that'd be really cool," said Lydia. "Imagine Fairies delivering bottles of clouds to Barn Owl just so she can make her special cloudy lemonade for us."

"I do so wish Fairies existed," said Amy, "I'd love to have one as a friend."

"Me too," said Lydia. "Imagine all the magical adventures you could have."

"We could visit Fairyland," said Amy.

"Ride a Unicorn," Lydia replied, "It'd be so much fun. Let's play Fairies next week, Amy." Lydia turned to Becca and Emma, "Would you like to come over to mine next week and we can play at being in Fairyland?"

Becca's hand found Emma's under the table and squeezed it. They looked at each other and the look said, 'Say nothing', but they both wondered if Amy was right and Barn Owl was friends with the

Fairies and she did get clouds delivered to her to make her special cloudy lemonade. There was no doubting that it was the best lemonade they'd ever tasted.

"We'd love to," Becca replied, "we can ask Mummy tomorrow when we're picked up."

"I think," said Freya, who had been listening to the girls talking of Witches and Fairies, "that Barn Owl made up the bit about real clouds in her lemonade to give us something to talk about, and it worked. She's not really a Witch at all, she doesn't really collect clouds and Fairies don't exit."

"How do you know they don't exist?" asked Lydia.

"Because if they did I would have seen one, and I haven't. Have you?"

"No..er..no, I don't think so."

"Well there you go, they don't exist."

Becca turned to Emma, "She sounds just like my brother," she whispered and they giggled.

At the far edge of the clearing where their campsite was a dozen Fairies flew out of the woods and flew around each other as though they were dancing.

From where the girls were sitting they looked just like butterflies but Becca and Emma, who saw them first, smiled with joy. They could see Sienna and

Rose, Cornflower, Violet, Lilac, Foxglove and several others.

"Go on," said Lily landing on Becca's shoulder and making her jump. She didn't even realise the tiny Fairy was in the campsite, let alone so close. "Point them out if you want to, but don't say what they are. Most of them will only see butterflies or dragonflies anyway."

"They might exist," said Becca to Freya.

"I think I'd know if I'd seen any," Freya replied.

"They might be really tiny," said Emma, and you might not be able to see them.

"Yes," Becca continued, "how do you know that those things flying over there by the trees aren't Fairies?" The girls looked across the clearing to where Becca was pointing. The Fairies continued spinning and weaving around each other in their playful dance, elegant and beautiful as they flew around, flying up and flying down.

Becca and Emma could make out each Fairy as she flew gracefully through the air, dancing in time with the others, flying fast and yet never touching.

The girls all looked across the glade. Some couldn't see what they were meant to be looking at and the others saw exactly what Lily had told Becca they would see; a dozen butterflies flying around the edge of the woods on a hot, sunny, summer afternoon.

"Wouldn't it be great if they really were Fairies," said Amy

"Oh yes," said Lydia, "really brilliant."

"They're just butterflies," said Freya

Lydia gazed at them longingly. They did look like butterflies from where the girls were sitting, watching them and yet, somehow, they didn't.

Was it the shape of their wings?

Or was it the way they moved?

It seemed that one or two of the other girls were having similar thoughts and a silence descended on them.

Slowly and silently, Lydia started to stand up, her eyes transfixed on the tiny creatures so far away. Ever so carefully she stepped over the bench she had been sitting on and took a small step towards the group of dancing Fairies. Then another, and another. She was walking so carefully that it seemed she was almost gliding across the grass. Seconds later she was joined by Amy. They couldn't take their eyes off the flying dancers that were playing together on the other side of the clearing.

It was as if a spell had been cast and Lydia and Amy were being drawn to the little group, who were darting this way and that before their eyes, like a troupe of tiny airborne dancers.

They were still a long way across the clearing but, as the two girls took another step, the Fairies suddenly flew off, back into the woods.

"See," said Freya, after a few moments, the spell that had held them all so transfixed, suddenly broken, "like I said, butterflies," and she turned back to the table.

"They didn't look like butterflies," said Lydia, quietly, fully believing that they might have seen Fairies; certainly, she wanted to believe that that was what they had seen, but there was still some doubt in her mind.

"Dragonflies then," said Freya. "Who cares?"

Becca and Emma, who had watched the Fairy dance and knew exactly what they had seen, were puzzled. Why had the Fairies shown themselves like that and then flown away so quickly? And why had Becca been told she could point them out if she wanted to? It seemed to the two girls that the Fairies wanted to be seen and yet didn't want to be seen and the girls were confused.

Lydia turned to Becca and she could see the excitement in her eyes.

"They looked like Fairies to me, Becca," she said in a whisper, not wanting the others to hear what she was saying and think she was silly. "They really did look like Fairies. Do you think Fairies really exist?"

"They looked like Fairies to me too," Becca replied honestly, and Emma nodded her head in agreement and smiled at Becca. They were both unsure whether they were meant to continue to keep it their secret or not, so they decided to keep the secret unless they were told otherwise.

"Who wants strawberries and cream?" boomed Brown Owl, striding across the field to where the girls' were sitting.

To cries of "me please," and "ooh, yes please," the girls ran over to the fire pit where Tawny Owl was busy filling paper bowls with handfuls of large, red strawberries.

"The cream is in those jugs at the end of the table," she said, "and don't forget to pick up a spoon, otherwise you'll have to come back and get one."

The strawberries were delicious, ripe and juicy, and it wasn't very long before every strawberry was eaten.

"Right girls," said Tawny Owl when everyone had finished, "Seconders will each come and get a black bin bag and throw away all the used plates and cups while the rest of you line up in your Sixes over there," she pointed to a spot about ten metres away from the pile of wood and sticks, then she strode back across the field and started walking around it.

The girls walked across the field, full up with the barbeque and the strawberries, towards the pile of sticks that would soon be a blazing bonfire. Becca and Emma were the last girls to arrive and they went to stand in their Six with Lydia and Amy. Lily and Cornflower appeared and flew alongside them.

"Ooh," said Lily, "fire can be very scary."

"Particularly in the wrong hands," added Cornflower.

"You should be very careful," Lily added.

"But Tawny Owl will be in control," said Becca.

"That's alright then," said Lily, "so long as there's a grown up looking after it."

"Pixies Sixer come and stand here," said Tawny Owl and she pointed to a piece of paper sticking out of the wood pile near to the ground, and Freya stood there as instructed.

"Sprites Sixer over here, Gnomes Sixer here and Elves Sixer stand here."

The Sixers were placed at four points around the fire so that they were each opposite another Sixer.

The sticks and twigs they had gathered earlier were neatly stacked up in front of them to create a bonfire that was nearly as tall as Tawny Owl, who now handed each of the Sixers a long, waxed stick.

"The Sixers now have a taper," she explained to everyone, "which is a little bit like a very thin candle. In a minute, I shall light the tapers, but before I do I'd like to remind you that fire can be dangerous if anyone is silly, so girls, you are not to stand any closer to the fire than you already are and Sixers, as soon as you have lit the bonfire you will walk, don't run, and stand with your Six. Please raise your hand if you do not understand."

No one raised their hand, they all knew how dangerous fire could be, they had been shown a film at school about how quickly fire can spread.

The other Brownie leaders, having cleared up and walked over and joined them, were also standing well away from the wood pile.

Tawny Owl went to each of the four Sixers and with a lighter she lit the taper in their hands.

"Sixers, you will see before you a piece of twisted paper sticking out of the fire just in front of you. When I say so you will set this piece of paper alight and walk to stand with your Six as the fire burns.

"Are you ready?"

"Yes, Tawny Owl," the Sixers replied.

"Right ho then, you may light the bonfire."

The four Sixers knelt down and touched their burning taper to the twist of paper sticking out of the wood pile. As each flame flared up they quickly, but carefully, stood up and walked away to join the other girls.

Each piece of paper burned brightly.

Then a strange thing happened.

It seemed as though a sudden breeze went swirling around the edge of the fire or, more specifically, around each flame, and blew it out.

Becca and Emma couldn't be sure but they were certain that the strange little winds were not natural, but rather the flames had deliberately been blown out by Fairies who had flown so fast that no one had been able to see them, not even Becca and Emma.

"How strange," said Tawny Owl, as she walked around the wood pile with a puzzled look on her face, "I've never seen that happen before. It's almost as if someone blew them out.

"Still," she continued, "we just have to try again."

Tawny Owl called the Sixers back and lit their tapers again and they stood around the wood pile as before.

"OK girls, light the fire," Tawny Owl instructed them and, once again, the Sixers knelt down and lit the twist of paper, making sure they were burning before stepping back to their Sixes.

They watched the flames flare as the paper burned and then, just as suddenly as before, an invisible wind swirled around each flame, putting it out and leaving a little plume of smoke twisting into the air and disappearing.

Becca saw a tiny blue blur in front of her and Lily suddenly appeared, out of breath and with a worried look on her little round face.

"What's the matter," Becca asked, "and why does our fire keep going out? Is it you?"

"You have to stop it," Lily gasped, "there's a baby hedgehog in the pile and it's trying to get out."

"Where?"

"Look at where Freya is trying to light the fire," Lily said.

"Yes."

"Are you looking?"

"Yes."

"Now look slightly to your left."

Becca looked to the left and, after a few moments, she saw a slight movement deep inside the wood pile. It was ever so slight, but once she had seen it she could see that there was something in there, something moving.

"Right Sixers," said Tawny Owl, "we'll try again."

Becca stuck her hand in the air.

"Please Tawny Owl?" she called out, and everyone turned and looked at her.

"Yes, Rebecca?" Tawny Owl said with her gentle smile.

"I think there's something in the wood pile and it's trying to get out."

"Really?"

"Yes, I think it may be a hedgehog," she continued, "look, there."

All the girls started crowding forward, looking into the wood pile to where Becca was pointing.

"Girls stand back," said Brown Owl, sharply, and everyone stood back.

The pack leaders joined Tawny Owl.

"Rebecca come over here please," said Brown Owl. "Now, where did you say you saw it?"

Becca stepped forward and crouched down in front of the wood pile, pointing.

"Just there," she said and she could see the creature moving, "it's quite a way in."

Tawny Owl and Snowy Owl crouched down beside her and peered into the pile. Snowy Owl had a torch in her pocket and she drew it out and shone the beam of light into the pile of sticks. She peered in, moving the beam around.

After what seemed ages, she gasped.

"You're right, Rebecca," she said, "I do believe there is a hedgehog in there. Tawny Owl, will you please help me while I reach in and see if I can rescue it?"

Becca and Emma watched Lily and Cornflower fly into the pile as Tawny Owl, helped by the other two pack leaders, held onto the sticks so the pile wouldn't collapse as Snowy Owl carefully pushed her hand, and then her arm, into the pile.

Her arm was in right up to her shoulder when she said, "yes, I think I've got it," and there was a scuffle in the pile.

"Ouch," said Snowy Owl, "its prickles are really sharp."

After several attempts to pick it up, Snowy Owl finally started pulling her arm out of the pile.

"Oops," she said, when she had pulled her arm out to her elbow, "I dropped it," and they all held their breath as she started searching with her hand once more.

"Ah, don't worry," she said after a few moments, "panic over, I've got it again," and everyone breathed a sigh of relief as Snowy Owl gently pulled her arm out of the wood pile. She stood up and turned to the girls who had gathered around her and she held up her hand and showed them a small hedgehog. It was only about the size of her hand and it was curled up into a ball, but everyone could see that it was just a baby.

"Now girls," said Snowy Owl, "do you know what I should do with this baby hedgehog?"

Lily, who had flown back out of the wood pile, perched on Becca's shoulder and whispered into her ear; "You should carefully place him on the ground, away from people, but not too far away as you don't want him to become lost."

"Anyone know?"

Becca and Emma, who had also heard what Lily had said, both hesitantly put up their hands.

Snowy Owl smiled at the two girls. "Yes, Rebecca, you saw him so what do you think we should do?"

Becca repeated what Lily had told her.

"That's exactly right, Rebecca, well done. Now, I'll take this little ball of prickles and put it down over here and, if we stay very still and very quiet, we will probably see him uncurl and run off."

With that she carried the little Hedgehog away from the girls, carefully put it down on the path a few metres away, and then returned to the others.

They watched with baited breath. No girl made a sound as they gazed at the ball of prickles lying motionless on the path in front of them.

Seconds passed that seemed like minutes. It seemed as though time had decided to stand still.

The girls didn't move.

The Hedgehog didn't move.

More seconds passed and then there was a slight movement and the Hedgehog uncurled just enough so that he could stick his nose out and carefully sniff the air. The girls could see his tiny pink nose twitching and then, a few moments later, sensing no danger, the little Hedgehog uncurled, rolled onto his front and scurried away from the girls. As he did so, the girls, who had managed to remain so quiet until then, burst into loud chatter as they started talking about what they had just seen, or about other Hedgehogs that they had seen in their gardens at home.

Chapter Six

Campfire Songs

At last Tawny Owl began to prepare the sixers for a third attempt at lighting the fire but, before they had a chance even to get their tapers lit again, there was a whoosh and a colourful blur around the bottom of the pile of wood and the twists of paper suddenly lit up and the flames grew bigger.

The twigs quickly caught, followed by the branches and very soon the whole pile was ablaze with flames licking noisily into the air.

Everyone looked on in silence, quite surprised by what they were seeing.

Tawny Owl turned to the girls, she looked a little shocked.

"See that girls?" she said, to the sound of the crackling flames behind her, "the fire was clearly still alight and just waiting to catch properly.

"As I said earlier, fire can be dangerous and unpredictable. We thought it had gone out when really it must have been still smouldering and look," and she turned to the point at the fire, "it's now roaring away."

And indeed, the fire was burning away merrily. It looked fantastic and the girls could feel its heat on their faces even from where they were standing.

"What happened just then?" asked Becca as Lily landed on her hand.

"We stopped the pile from catching fire to save the little Hedgehog," she replied. "We used magic to do that and, when the Hedgehog was safe and all you humans were safely away from the fire, we released the magic spell and the fire was able to burn again."

"It was a bit scary the way it suddenly burst into flames when we all thought it had gone out," said Emma

"I'm not sure I like fire that much anymore," said Becca.

"You were all safe," said Cornflower who was sitting on Emma's shoulder, "we wouldn't have let any harm come to you or your pack leaders, but fire can be dangerous, even for us Fairies, if we're not careful."

As the smell of burning wood and leaves wafted over the girls they all sat down and Barn Owl come over with her guitar.

Everyone knows that Brownies love to sing songs around the campfire and the girls were all excitedly looking forward to singing some of their favourite campfire songs.

"What's happening now?" asked Lily, watching Barn Owl sit down on an old tree stump facing the girls and start to turn the keys at the end of her guitar.

"We're going to sing some songs," Becca told her. "Campfire songs."

"Ooh, we love singing, don't we Cornflower?"

"Yes, yes, yes, we do," her sister replied, "We're really good at singing."

"You're always good at everything until you do it," said Emma with a laugh, "like hide-and-seek."

Barn Owl strummed her fingers across the strings.

The chord rang out sweet and pure and Barn Owl smiled.

"Right girls," she said, playing another, different, chord, "to warm us all up we'll start with an old favourite, 'Campfire's Burning'. We'll sing it through two times first of all and then we'll sing it in a round," and she went on to explain what a round was and where each six would sing the song.

The song would start with one six singing the first line and when they started singing the second line the next six would start with the first line and so on so that, when the first six was singing the fourth line the fourth six would be just starting to sing the first line.

With the sun shining on her face and the orange and red flames of the fire licking high into the air behind her, Barn Owl looked like an angel to the girls as she strummed her guitar and the soft chords echoed around the clearing.

A pack leader came and sat with each six. They said it was to help them but really it was because, like the girls, they love to sing campfire songs as well.

"I'll count you in for four," said Barn Owl over the sound of the chords, then we'll start. Remember we'll sing it through together two times, then Pixies will sing the first line on their own, then Sprites will join in, followed by Gnomes and finally Elves will sing. We'll sing it through as a round three times.

"Ready, and one, two, three, four..." and they all started singing 'Campfire's Burning."

At first Becca and Emma were put off by Lily and Cornflower singing in their ears. Their high pitched little voices sounded quite beautiful together and Becca and Emma quickly got used to them so that by the time they were singing together for the second time around they were able to sing along quite happily.

"Now, Pixies only" said Barn Owl when they had sung it through twice and the Pixies started singing the first line of the song with the help of Brown Owl, who had a very loud, booming sort of voice when she was singing, that was much deeper than the rest of them.

"Now Sprites start," said Barn Owl as Pixies started singing the second line, and the Sprites sang the first line over the Pixies who were singing the second line. The Gnomes and Elves joined in when it was their turn and soon each six was singing a different line.

It was ever so much fun and no-one made any mistakes at all.

They were in full voice, smiling as they sang, when the Pixies sang, 'Come sing and be merry' for the last time and they could listen to the other sixes sing and, in turn, stop until just the Elves were singing the last line and then there was silence.

All the girls let out a loud cheer and clapped their perfect round as their leaders congratulated them all.

"That was fun," Lily said, "can we do it again?"

"Shh," said Becca, "we'll sing another song now."

"Which one?"

"Dunno," Becca replied, "wait and see."

"Wait and see? Now you sound like your Mummy," said Lily with a laugh.

"Now we'll sing 'Animal Fair', said Barn Owl, "and we'll start by everyone singing 'monkey-monkey-monkey-monkey'."

Following Barn Owl they all started chanting 'monkey-monkey-monkey-monkey' over and over.

"Right Gnomes, you sing the verse," said Barn Owl and the Gnomes sang, "The animals held a fair, the birds and bees were there," as the other girls continued to sing 'monkey-monkey-monkey-monkey'. It was perfect and when the Gnomes sang the last line, 'and what became of the monkey-monkey-monkey-monkey," they were all in time with the others, and then it was turn of the Elves to sing it.

"You do have some funny songs," said Cornflower, when they had finished 'Animal Fair', and everyone had had a turn at singing the verse, "but they are jolly good fun."

"And we learned them ever so quickly," added Lily.

Barn Owl had them singing a version of 'Pizza Hut' next and followed by 'Kookaburra' and then they sang 'In a Cottage in the Wood,' and did all the actions of the old man at the window, the huntsman shooting and the old man comforting the rabbit he had saved.

After a few more songs they came to the last one.

"Who knows 'I'm a Thousand-Legged Worm?' asked Barn Owl.

Most of the girls put their hands up, jumping to be seen and to show everyone that they knew it. Only a few of the newer Brownies didn't know it.

"Right, we'll start by making a circle," and all the girls jumped up and eventually, once everyone had sorted out who they were going to stand next to, they were all stood in a circle.

"Now, Freya will step inside the circle and everyone else close the gap."

After they had shuffled together again Freya was standing inside the circle.

"When we sing the verse," Barn Owl continued, "you girls in the circle will walk around in this direction," and she pointed to the right, "and Freya will walk in the other direction," and she pointed left. "OK?"

All the girls nodded their heads enthusiastically.

"And when we start singing the chorus you will all stop and Freya will turn and face whoever she is opposite in the circle and both girls will hop on one leg and sing the chorus together.

"When you've sung the chorus the girl who was hopping with Freya will join her inside the circle and we'll do it all again and this time there will be two pairs of girls singing the chorus as they hop, then four pairs until you are all in the centre and the song is over.

"Let's give it a try."

Barn Owl started playing her guitar again and the girls all started walking around in the circle with Freya on the inside, then Barn Owl counted them in and they all started singing the song.

When they got to the chorus Freya was opposite Beth and the two of them turned to face each other. They both lifted one leg and started hopping as they tried to sing the chorus on their own. It was so funny as they struggled to keep their balance, sing, hop and not laugh all at the same time and the other girls clapped and laughed with them. They were all having such a good time.

They finally finished the chorus and now Beth and Freya were inside the circle and they started again.

This time when they got to the chorus Freya and Beth stopped opposite Becca and Emma. Lily and Cornflower hid so they weren't seen. Becca could feel Lily wriggling in her pocket and it tickled. As the four of them faced each other and hopped on one leg, Lily's tickling made Becca start giggling and, to the delight of everyone else, she lost her balance and fell over.

"Are you alright?" she whispered to Lily, worried in case she had squashed the little Fairy in her pocket.

"Yes," came the reply, "I don't squash that easily.

"Stop tickling me," she whispered, "you made me fall over."

"Sorry, I'll keep still as anything."

A big cheer went up and Becca quickly stood up and they continued the chorus where they had stopped, with the four girls hopping and singing until Becca and Emma were able to join Freya and Beth in the middle of the circle and they started again.

Very soon there were more girls inside the circle than outside and they were singing the chorus for the last time as every Brownie hopped on one leg and sang as loudly as they could after which they all fell to the ground in a heap, puffing and panting, laughing and shouting, clapping and gasping for breath.

"Oh," said Becca, lying on the ground beside Emma, "that was so much fun."

"Yes," puffed Emma, "so much fun."

"We enjoyed it too," said Cornflower, "and we're going off to teach all the songs to the others and have our own campfire singing," and off they flew into the wood as the girls got their breath back to start the next activity.

Chapter Seven

The Nature Trail

The sun was low in the sky casting long shadows of the trees over the campsite as four groups of girls, each led by a Brownie Pack leader, headed off along the woodland paths at the start of the nature trail.

The nature trail was always the highlight of the pack holiday weekend and, if it was a success, they would get to see rabbits, squirrels, various birds and maybe, as dusk fell, a real barn owl.

Before setting off the girls had been given a sheet of paper with a list of animals that they might see if they were very, very lucky. As well as the expected rabbits, sparrows, Blue Tits and Squirrels the list also included Foxes, Badgers, Stoats and Weasels but, as Brown Owl had pointed out, these animals were quite rare and very shy and so they were unlikely to see them.

The four groups of girls set off in different directions from the campsite so as not to have one large group that made too much noise and scared off any animals that may be out there. The girls of Pixies Six followed Brown Owl along the path, chattering away excitedly until Brown Owl stopped and turned to them.

"If you want to see any animals this evening," she said, quite sternly, "then you will have to be absolutely silent. I know you are all excited and it's difficult to keep quiet for very long but you must make a big effort as I will not keep stopping to tell you and anyone who makes too much noise will be sent back to the camp.

"Do I make myself clear?"

Becca and Emma gulped. Both their Mummies called them little chatterboxes and they rarely stopped talking for very long. Becca's Mummy once said she thought Becca must be breathing through her ears as she was talking so much.

"Yes, Brown Owl," the girls replied and Brown Owl smiled her big friendly smile at them and they set off at a happy pace.

It was very quiet in the woods. A slight breeze rustled through the branches above them and the surrounding woods was beginning to get gloomy as the sun sank slowly towards the horizon.

It was as though the whole wood had heard Brown Owl's stern words and was now holding its breath and trying not to make a sound.

The way the shadows of the branches moved across the woodland path in the gathering gloom was quite spooky and Becca and Emma held each other's hand as they walked along at the back of the group, each feeling just a little bit scared.

They squeezed their hands together, feeling comforted as they walked on behind the others in silence.

The evening was warm and, as the light was gradually fading, the girls' excitement grew.

What would be the first animal they saw on the nature trail, they wondered.

With their eyes wide all the girls of Pixies Six looked carefully around them as they walked along, peering into the surrounding woods and along the path, each hoping to be the first so see an animal. Occasionally Becca and Emma would turn right around, just in case any animal tried to sneak across the path behind them.

Brown Owl stopped and turned to face the girls.

"Don't be worried if we don't see anything immediately," she whispered, "the daytime animals and birds are just getting ready to go to bed and the night-time ones are just getting up and aren't out yet, but don't worry, they'll come, I'm quite sure." And with that, she turned and continued walking along the path.

"I hope she's right," Becca whispered, trying to be as quiet as she could, "it'll be a very boring walk if we don't see anything."

"I hope we don't meet anything dangerous," Emma replied, as quietly as possible.

"Like what?"

"I dunno. Wolves?"

"Don't be silly, we don't have wolves in this country."

"Are you sure?"

"Yes, we definitely don't."

"But I've often heard Daddy say he's working hard to keep the wolves from the door."

"I don't know what he means because we don't have any."

"Good."

"The wildest animal we have in this country is probably a Fox and I don't think they're very dangerous."

"I'd love to see a Fox, they're ever so cute."

As they were talking their voices were steadily getting louder and before they knew it they had bumped into Brown Owl who was looking at them with a stern look on her face.

"What did I say?" said Brown Owl.

"We're sorry, Brown Owl," the girls said together. They were horrified that they had been talking so loudly.

"Keep your voices down," Brown Owl told them, "or better still, don't talk at all. Your voices carry at this time of day and any animal can hear you coming from miles way. You'll scare them off."

Becca and Emma looked down at their feet as Brown Owl told them off and Becca fought tears.

Then Brown Owl, who was really ever so nice, laughed and put her arms around the two sad little girls and said, "If chattering was an Olympic sport you two would win gold medals every time. Now Rebecca and Emma, do try and be as quiet as you can or I'll have to split you up so you can't chitter-chatter with each other all the time."

Still whispering herself, Brown Owl turned.

"Follow me," she said, "and Rebecca and Emma can walk with me.

With Becca and Emma walking alongside Brown Owl, with Brown Owl in the middle and holding their hands, the girls of Pixie Six walked on in silence, still looking carefully about for any signs of wildlife.

They walked.

And they walked.......

And they walked.......

But there was no sign of any animal or bird and the woods remained silent.

"I wish Lily was here," Becca thought to herself as she walked silently beside Brown Owl, "this is so boring."

"Hello!" whispered a tiny voice in her ear, "what are you doing?"

Becca nearly jumped out of her skin as Lily flew in front of her, pulled a funny face and flew back onto her shoulder.

"Don't say anything," Lily whispered in her ear, "I can hear your thoughts."

"We're doing a nature trail," Becca thought.

"What's a nature trail?" Lily replied and, as Becca thought of the answer Lily whispered, "Oh, I see. But there's no animals to see?"

"How do you do that?" Becca suddenly said out loud, and then put her free hand to her mouth.

She looked up at Brown Owl. "I'm sorry."

Brown Owl, who had been walking along slowly and being very careful not to tread on any sticks or twigs, was looking up at the trees and letting out a strange whistling noise which sounded like a birdcall of some kind.

Thinking that Becca was talking to her and asking about her bird call she looked down and smiled.

"When I was young," she said in her soft voice, "I learned how to make certain bird calls. That one was a blackbird. I was trying to make the forest animals think there's a blackbird singing so they don't get scared by us."

A burst of high pitched laughter sounded in Becca's left ear and Becca could feel Lily jumping up and down on her shoulder.

"They don't think she's a blackbird," Lily gasped, "she sounds nothing like a blackbird."

"Wow," said Emma, "can you really sing like a blackbird?"

"No, she can't," Lily gasped, struggling to control her laughter.

"What other ones can you do?" Becca asked, trying to ignore Lily's rude outburst.

"I can do a thrush," said Brown Owl and made a whistling noise that, to Becca's ears, sounded very like a real bird call.

Lily's laughing burst out again, even louder than before and Becca looked at Lily who was now lying on her back on Becca's shoulder, holding her tummy and kicking her legs in the air.

"That's ..." she said, "hahaha, that's so ... hahaha ... funny ... hahaha ... she ... (gasp) ... thinks ... hahaha ... she sounds .... Oh, my goodness ... like ... hahaha ... a thrush."

Becca glared at Lily and thought, as loud as she could, "Shhh! You shouldn't be so rude. She might hear you. Anyway, she sounds good to me."

Lily immediately stopped laughing and stood up. She had a sorrowful look on her face.

"Sorry," she whispered and, clinging to Becca's neck, she kissed Becca lightly on the cheek. "I'm not allowed to be rude, are you cross with me?"

"Not really," thought Becca after a few moments pause, "but Brown Owl is ever so nice to us."

Lily sat down on Becca's shoulder as they continued their walk.

"Can you read my mind all the time?" Becca thought to Lily.

"Oh no," said Lily. "Only when I think you want me to hear what you are thinking."

"But how do you know if you're not listening?"

"I just do," Lily replied, "I'm a Fairy, I have magic. I know when you want me to hear your thoughts and I know when you don't.

"Well I wish" Becca began to say …

".. that you and Cornflower could magic up some animals for us to see, this walk is really boring," said Lily, finishing Becca's sentence for her as she thought it.

Becca gasped and looked at Lily. Lily leapt off Becca's shoulder, flew in front of her, gave her a sweet smile and winked at her. Lily's big smile always made Becca happy and she turned as Lily flew off into the trees.

"What's the matter Rebecca?" asked Brown Owl feeling Becca's hand tugging on her own as Becca turned to watch her Fairy fly away, "Did you see anything?"

"Sorry Brown Owl, I was just looking to see if I could see something."

"Good girl," replied the Brownie leader, "keep looking. And did you see anything?"

"No."

Brown Owl stopped and they all looked around. The only wildlife to be seen right then was a large swarm of gnats that was flying around an old tree stump at the edge of the path. The girls ensured they kept as far away from the swarm as possible as none of them wanted to be bitten.

"Well," said Brown Owl, scratching her head and looking a little confused, "it seems as though all the animals in this wood are being very lazy this evening and none of them want to come out and play. At least, they don't want to play for us."

The girls let out a disappointed groan.

"Still," Brown Owl continued, forcing herself to smile, "we're only halfway along the nature trail and anything can happen. Who knows," she said, looking at each girl individually with an enthusiastic clap of her hands, "we might see so many animals in the next half an hour that we won't have time to count them all."

As she spoke two small bats flew out of the trees, darting this way and that across the path and over towards the tree stump where the cloud of gnats was still flying.

The girls watched in fascination as the two bats flew back and forth over the stump.

"As you can see," Brown Owl whispered in a voice so quiet that the girls had to listen hard to hear what she was saying, "the two bats are flying into the swarm of gnats that are flying over that tree stump. Bats eat insects and that's why we like them so much.

"Who can tell me anything about bats?"

"They're not birds," said Freya, "but flying animals."

"That's right Freya," said Brown Owl, "they're actually flying mammals. Anything else?"

"My dad says they're protected so you're not allowed to kill them," said Lydia.

"That's right, Lydia. Do you know why they are protected?"

"Because they're pretty?"

"Because they only come out at night?"

"Because there's not many left?"

The answers all came together as all the girls offered up an idea.

"It's because, in this country, there's not many left," said Brown Owl. "They are what's known as an endangered species, which means that there's so few of them left that they are in danger of disappearing completely if we don't do something to help them. That's why they are protected."

As Brown Owl was explaining this to the girls they all became aware that the woods had come alive with noise. They heard birds chirping, leaves rustling and, in the distance, they heard the barking of a fox.

A family of blue tits flew across the clearing just ahead of them and gathered on the branch of a tree overhanging the path.

The girls all pulled out their nature trail sheet and placed a tick against Blue Tit. Becca saw Emma write 'Bat' at the bottom of her piece of paper as it wasn't on the list. Becca copied Emma and wrote 'Bat' on her own sheet.

"I asked Lily if the Fairies could magic up some animals for us to see," she whispered to Emma, "and it looks like they have."

"I hope they get some really exciting animals for us," her friend replied, "I'd love to see a Fox or a Badger."

There was a rustling in the bush near to where they were standing and they heard a shrill whistle. Sitting on a large stone beneath a leaf in the undergrowth was Sienna.

"You shall see some animals," she told the girls, "Lily and Cornflower are off talking to them at the moment. You must promise not to hurt or scare any of them and not to be frightened by any of them."

"We promise," they both replied and Sienna held out her hands to them. They knelt down and they both stretched out a finger to gently touch Sienna's hand.

"Look out for a Field Mouse, which will come out right here as soon as I go," Sienna continued, "and as you walk along the path a short while you will see a Grass Snake on its way to find somewhere to sleep."

"Ooh, fab," said Becca as Sienna flew away.

Seconds later, exactly as Sienna had promised, a tiny field mouse appeared climbing up the branch of the bramble.

"Brown Owl," Becca whispered, as loud as she could without actually shouting, "look!"

"What is it Rebecca?" Brown Owl asked, hearing the excitement in Becca's voice and crossing the path to where the two girls were crouched over a bush.

120

"It's a Field Mouse," Emma whispered, not wanting to take her eye off the tiny creature.

"Oh wonderful," Brown Owl said, "show me."

Becca pointed to the branch on which the mouse was sitting looking at them and the rest of the girls from Pixie Six quickly and quietly gathered around to see.

The little mouse sat there, quietly, staring at them. It calmly started to wash its face and whiskers, wiping its paw around its ear and then cocked its head to one side.

It let out a little squeak as it looked at them, then pulled at a red berry on the branch just in front of it. The berry came away from the branch and the mouse, holding the berry with both its paws, nibbled at it, rapidly turning it as it hungrily ate it all up.

Sitting upon its hind legs, it sniffed the air, then turned and leapt back into the undergrowth.

The girls and Brown Owl had watched in silence, some had even held their breath and, as soon as the little mouse was gone it was as if a spell had been broken and there were gasps of "Wow!" and "Totes brill," as the girls all suddenly started to talk at once.

"Well that was lucky," said Brown Owl, as they all stood up, ready to continue the nature trail with fresh excitement, "well done to Rebecca and Emma for spotting that little beauty."

Becca and Emma smiled, it made them both feel good when they were praised by Brown Owl.

"Now," Brown Owl continued, "let's see what other animals we can find in this lovely wood."

The sun was sinking lower in the sky as they started walking again and the path was now quite gloomy. Even so, they could still see quite clearly and Becca and Emma kept their eyes open looking for the grass snake that Sienna had promised, and hoping that it hadn't already passed as they had been so long watching the mouse.

The woods seemed alive now as dusk fell.

"Listen to all those birds chattering as they start to roost," said Brown Owl.

"Please Brown Owl, what does roost mean?" asked Amy.

"When birds settle down for the night to go to sleep it's called roosting," Brown Owl explained. "It's just what we call the way they sleep."

The path they were on had reached the wall which marked the edge of the Florence Walker Memorial Centre and it turned to the left. Walking along the wall a short way Becca and Emma, who were currently walking ahead of the others, spotted the movement in front of them and stopped as the head of the grass snake peeped out from the undergrowth and started slithering across the path.

The others stopped behind them and they heard Amy ask in a whisper, "what have you seen this time?"

Staying ever so quiet and without taking her eyes off the beautiful Grass Snake slithering slowly in front of them, she pointed out the creature to her friends and she heard their sharp intake of breath as they all caught sight of the snake.

The snake was green in colour with a bright yellow collar just behind its head. It had black markings all along its side and its body glistened when it was caught in the low rays of the sun. They could see the snake's forked tongue flicking out from its mouth as it slithered slowly across the path, zig-zagging. Its movement was so smooth and the girls watched it in silence.

"Golly," said Lydia, "it's ever so long."

And it was. The Grass Snake making its way across the path at the far end of the campsite was the largest snake in the woods and was nearly a metre long.

"Do you see the yellow marking just behind its head?" whispered Brown Owl, and the girls all nodded. "Well that, and its green colour, is how we know it is a harmless Grass Snake and not an Adder. Also, Adders don't grow to such a length," she added.

It was an exciting moment as none of the girls had ever seen a Grass Snake before, at least not one in the wild. Some of them had seen one at a zoo but this was special. This was a real snake in a real wood, not one in a glass tank that did nothing but curl up and sleep.

The Grass Snake was so long that as its head disappeared into the undergrowth on one side of the path its tail was still hidden in the undergrowth on the other side.

Its movement was so graceful and for a while, whilst its head was hidden in the undergrowth on one side of the path and its tail hidden in the other side, they had to really concentrate on it to see that it was moving at all.

They watched as, at last, its tail crossed the path and then it was gone. Its tail disappeared into the grass where its head had entered moments earlier and, try as they might, they could hear no sound from it as it slithered away and continued its journey into the wood where it would eventually curl up and, as the temperature fell, fall asleep until the warmth of the morning sun warmed it up enough to wake up and continue its journey.

The girls pulled out their Nature Trail work sheet. Grass Snake was not on their list so Brown Owl told them to add it in and tick it off.

"How lucky we all are to see a Grass Snake," said Brown Owl. "Although they are not endangered they are very shy creatures and will always avoid humans whenever they can, so it is quite a treat to see one, especially one as beautiful as that one was."

The girls of Pixies Six walked on through the woods. The path was long and winding as it trailed through the woods, but it was designed so that the girls could walk from any of the camping areas and eventually arrive back to where they started. That way there was no chance that anyone could get lost.

Chapter Eight

Bunnies; Badgers and Barn Owls

"This is getting to be fun," said Becca to Emma.

"Thanks to Lily and Cornflower," Emma replied.

"And Sienna," added Lily.

"Oh my goodness," exclaimed Becca, "I didn't know you were there. You made me jump."

"I'm here too," said Cornflower, making the two girls jump again, which made the two Fairies giggle.

"Don't forget Rose, Hyacinth, Petunia, Foxglove and Primrose," she added, "they're all helping too."

The Fairies had been busy and in the space of just a few minutes the girls had seen Bats, Blue Tits, a Field Mouse and a Grass Snake, and there was still plenty of time left on the walk to see more.

Suddenly the Nature Trail was no longer boring but had become quite exiting and really interesting.

"Thank you," said Becca and Emma together.

"Thank you so much, you made this walk really brilliant," added Becca.

"I wonder what we're going to see next?" Emma whispered.

"Oh, that's easy," said Lily.

"Rabbits," said Cornflower.

"Hey, I was going to tell them that," Lily said crossly, pushing her sister.

"I love Rabbits," said Emma, "I would love to have a Rabbit, but Mummy won't let me have one."

"It's not fair," said Becca.

"Why not?" asked Cornflower.

"She says 'why do you need one of your own when there are so many in the woods already?'"

"She's right," said Cornflower.

"Why?" asked Emma.

"You shouldn't keep a wild animal in a cage when it should be running around the woods."

"Well, I haven't got one," said Emma, "so I can't."

"Me neither," said Becca.

Lydia suddenly told everyone to shush in a loud voice.

She blushed as everyone stopped and looked at her, expectantly.

"Something moved," she whispered.

"Where?" asked Freya.

"Just the other side of that tree," she replied.

They all gathered together by the tree.

On the other side, just away from the woodland path, was a grassy clearing, and in the clearing, lolloping around and eating the grass, was a colony of a dozen Rabbits. They were light brown in colour with black tips on the ends of their long ears.

"Look," whispered Lydia, who was ever so pleased that she had been the one who discovered the little colony, "babies."

They all followed the direction of Lydia's finger as she pointed and there, at the far end of the clearing and close to the entrance to their warren, were four of the cutest little baby Rabbits the girls had ever seen.

They were so sweet and the girls just wanted to pick them up and cuddle them, but they remained hidden so as not to scare them away.

One of the little ones suddenly leapt into the air, jumped over one of the other babies and charged across the clearing. The other three charged after it, as though they were playing a game of tag, and they all landed in a heap just by the tree where the girls of Pixies Six were gathered.

Becca and Emma caught a glimpse of a tiny Fairy flying into the woods. She had been just where the first little rabbit has been sitting.

The adult Rabbits casually looked up at the playing youngsters and, seeing that they were playing rather than running from any danger, carried on eating.

As quietly as they could, so as not to disturb the family of rabbits, the girls withdrew and gathered around Brown Owl.

"Well," she said to the girls, "this is already turning out to be one of the best Nature Trails I've ever done. What a lucky evening we are having. I wonder if we'll see anything else."

"I do hope so," said Amy, turning to Becca and Emma, "I'm so enjoying this."

"Me too," said Lydia as they all followed after Brown Owl.

"It's because you've all been so quiet," said Brown Owl, still keeping her voice down to a whisper and looking pointedly at Becca. Becca blushed and smiled back. "And if you continue to keep quiet then I am sure we'll see some more."

As she paused and looked at the six excited faces in front of her an eerie screech echoed through the woods.

The girls huddled together as they heard another screech. In the gloom of the woodland path the screeching noise sounded ghostly. In their minds the girls pictured all sorts of wild beasts chasing them through the woods, trying to catch them before they got to the safety of the camp.

"Listen to that," said Brown Owl, "does anyone know what animal made that noise?"

Their initial fright at the noise had gone and the girls listened. Above the general noise of the twittering birds they heard the screech again.

"Is it an owl?" asked Beth.

"Yes, Beth," said Brown Owl. "It makes quite a scary noise doesn't it?"

The girls all smiled, feeling a bit silly for being scared when they first heard it.

"Now, does anyone know what type of owl makes that noise?"

"A Brown Owl?" said Beth.

Brown Owl laughed softly and smiled at Beth.

"No dear," she said, "a Brown Owl goes 'twit-twoo'"

"Is it a Barn Owl?" asked Becca, who quite often heard similar screeching noises when she was lying in bed in summer with her bedroom window open.

"That's right Rebecca, that's the screeching of a Barn Owl," said Brown Owl, "the screech seems to be coming from the trees in front of us, over that way. Let's quietly walk on; you never know, we might see it." And as they turned they saw, flying along the path in front of them, silent and ghost like as it glided through the air just a few feet above them, the Barn Owl that had been screeching as it flew through the woods.

As it approached them they could see its huge eyes in its pointy round white face. The Barn Owl flew along the path between the trees, slowly turning its head and looking to the left and right as it flew along. Occasionally it flapped it mighty wings in a slow motion which made no noise in the quiet of the surrounding woodland.

As they watched it the girls held their breath so as not to disturb the graceful bird. The owl rose up before them and hovered in the air a few feet in front of them. For what seemed like ages it hung in the air, its wings beating silently to keep it there, and stared at the group of girls below it.

Then it stopped flapping and, with its wings fully extended, suddenly dropped down towards them. The girls ducked down as it swooped low over their heads and Amy let out a little scream, then giggled in her embarrassment. As the owl gathered speed it gave a single flap of its wings and rose high into the air and flew on along the woodland path.

As it flew past them Becca and Emma saw, holding onto its back, six little Fairies, Lily; Cornflower; Sienna; Rose; Petunia and Primrose, all clearly enjoying their ride as if they

were riding on a rollercoaster. The Fairies looked at Becca and Emma and waved at them, shouting with joy in their little high-pitched voices. They all had big grins on their faces.

"Golly gosh," exclaimed Brown Owl breathlessly as she watched the Barn Owl disappear into the gathering gloom of the woods, "I've never seen anything like that before."

"That was so exciting," said Freya, as she stood up straight again.

There were various exclamations of 'Wow!'; and 'Brill!'; and 'Did you see that…!' as the girls started chattering, speaking rapidly as they talked about the flight of the Owl.

"Did you see the Fairies riding on its back?" Becca whispered to Emma.

"Yes," Emma replied, "they did that for us, you know."

"I love our Fairies."

But before they could talk any further Brown Owl called the girls to be quiet and gather around her.

They could all tell that Brown Owl was as excited by what had just happened as they were and she looked along the path to where the owl had flown as though she wished it would fly back again, but it was gone.

In the distance they heard it screech one last time and then the woods fell into an eerie silence for a brief moment. Then, as if someone had suddenly turned up the volume they could hear the general woodland noises once again.

"Let's all take a moment to get our breath back," said Brown Owl, "and then we will start heading back to camp."

The girls started to talk again in the same excited tones as before but Brown Owl raised a finger to her lips and they quickly fell silent again.

As Becca looked around her she noticed, right down at ground level, a tiny red door in the wall. It was half hidden by the leaves but she could see it clearly. She nudged Emma and pointed it out to her and, as they watched, the door opened and, much to their delight, Lily and Cornflower stepped out and flew up to them.

"Thank you," said Becca, "thank you both so much. You've made the Nature Trail really good fun."

"And please thank the others too," added Emma.

"Oh, we were having lots of fun too," replied Lily, "did you see us on the back of that Barn Owl. We did wave to you, you know."

"Yes, we saw you waving," said Becca. "Did the Owl let you ride him like that?"

"He's our friend," said Cornflower, "and he loves giving us Fairies a ride."

"We're ever so light," added Lily with a smile, "he hardly even notices we're there."

"We've got some more surprises," said Cornflower, bobbing about in front of them.

"Really," gasped Becca unable to hide the excitement in her voice.

"What?" asked Emma, jumping up and down and clapping her hands together.

"You'll see," said Lily, as the two Fairies flew up into the air. "You'll see."

"Look in the clearing just behind the next tree," said Cornflower as they flew off into the woods.

"What are you two doing?" asked Brown Owl as the two girls watched the disappearing Fairies, "and who were you talking to?"

"No one, Brown Owl," said Emma.

"We just thought we heard a noise. It was coming from behind that tree," Becca told her, "and we were going to see what it was."

"What sort of a noise?" asked Brown Owl.

"We don't really know," said Becca, "a sort of snuffly, shuffly, gruffly sort of a noise."

"We were just going to look and see," added Emma.

With Brown Owl between them they stepped off the woodland path and stood beside the tree. On the other side was a large clearing and across the other side of the clearing lay the trunk of a fallen tree.

By its side there were piles of earth that had been there for some time and they could see, beneath the trunk, a large, dark entrance to what looked like quite a deep hole.

The clearing was empty.

And silent.

Disappointed, they were just about to turn away when a movement from the tunnel entrance caught Becca's eye.

"Look," she whispered as quietly as she could and pointed at the fallen tree trunk.

As she spoke a black and white snout poked up from the dark entrance, twitching as it sniffed the air, checking for any strange scents. Long white whiskers on either side of the shiny black nose sprang forward followed by the head and body of a large Badger as it cautiously emerged from the hole, closely followed by two more, slightly smaller ones and then two cubs.

As the two cubs started to play together another one, smaller than the first two, poked its head out of the entrance to the set and slowly ventured into the clearing. It stood there shaking, as though it was frightened of being outside.

"It's probably the first time it has been outside," whispered Brown Owl to the girls, who were watching with baited breath.

The little cub had only taken a few steps when the other two cubs jumped on it and together the three of them rolled and tumbled across the grassy woodland floor.

For a moment it looked as though the Badger cubs were having a serious fight as they were growling and snarling at each other and bits of their fur were flying around as they tumbled together across the clearing, and even though the smallest one was being jumped on by the other two larger ones Brown Owl explained that they really were just playing.

"They seem very rough," said Freya who, with all the other girls, had joined Becca, Emma and Brown Owl to watch the Badgers playing.

"Look at their teeth," said Lydia, "they're huge."

"So are their claws," added Amy.

The claws on the Badgers' paws were long and they looked very sharp as they continued to play fight, rolling over and over and wriggling and jumping, kicking up a cloud of dust. As they snarled at each other they bared their teeth and they attempted to bite one another but they didn't seem to hurt themselves.

It was a wonderful sight and the girls were transfixed as they watched the Badgers playing until the small one finally broke free from the other two and bounded across the clearing where it snuggled up to one of the adult Badgers.

"Aw look," said Lydia, "he's run to his Mummy."

"He'll be safe there," said Amy, and it certainly seemed that he was because the other two kept away from the adult Badger who was now licking her baby as he lay down in front of her.

"Goodness," said Brown Owl, as they left the Badger family to play in peace, "I've never seen real Badgers in the wild before."

"Really?" asked Becca.

"I've only ever seen them on television before," she told them. "Just wait until I tell the other Pack Leaders, they'll be so jealous. That's if they haven't seen some too, of course."

Brown Owl looked at her watch.

"Come on girls, we'd better be getting back to camp. The others will be wondering what's happened to us."

"Maybe they'll think we've been eaten by a wild animal," said Amy, as they followed Brown Owl along the path once more. The girls giggled but Brown Owl wasn't going to tell them off now, they'd had such a fantastic evening.

As Becca and Emma returned to the path Lily and Cornflower appeared before them.

"Did you enjoy that?" asked Lily.

"Oh yes, thank you," Becca and Emma said together.

"We saved the best for last," added Cornflower.

"Wow, you certainly did," said Emma, "those Badgers were really fab."

"No," said Cornflower, with a puzzled look on her face, "when we say we saved the best for last ..."

"We mean," continued Lily, "that we saved the best for last. The best is still to come."

Becca and Emma both gasped.

"You mean ..." Emma started to say,

"... that the Badgers weren't the last?" Becca finished Emma's sentence.

"Yes," said Lily, "that's exactly what we mean."

"Oh, golly," squeaked Emma in delight, "what can be better than those Badgers?"

"You'll see," said Cornflower, and once again, the two Fairies flew off before the girls could ask them any more questions.

"What do you think we'll see next?" said Becca to Emma as they hurried to catch up with the others who had walked on ahead of them.

Brown Owl looked back and saw that they had trailed behind.

"Come on you slowcoaches," she said in her kindly voice as Becca and Emma ran to catch them up. Becca didn't think Brown Owl could ever be cross.

Brown Owl, Freya, Beth, Lydia and Amy had all turned around to watch Becca and Emma running along the path and so they didn't see the mighty Stag leap onto the path at the top of the sloping path ahead.

Becca and Emma saw him and stopped, staring in surprise.

"Oh my goodness," gasped Becca.

"Wow," exclaimed Emma.

"What is it?" asked Brown Owl.

"Look behind you," said Becca pointing beyond them and they all turned to see what Becca was pointing at.

The Stag stood there, in the middle of the path, with his head held high, blocking their way ahead. His huge antlers made him look magnificent as he was silhouetted against the red of the setting sun behind him. He stood proud and tall as he looked at them.

With a shake of his head the Stag pored at the ground with his front hoof and then, with a mighty leap, he bounded towards them.

"Quick, stand back," said Brown Owl, urgently. They could hear panic in her voice and she quickly pushed the girls behind her and stood, protectively, between them and the Stag, frightened that he might attack them. As the Stag reached them he stopped. For what seemed like ages, he stood looking at them. There was no fear in his eyes and he snorted quietly and tilted his head to one side.

Slowly, he walked towards them and Brown Owl backed away, holding her arms out to try and hide the girls. She did not want to make any sudden movement in case she caused the Stag to panic.

"Shooo!" she whispered. There was fear in her voice. Her fear was for the safety of the children rather than of the Stag. The Stag was beautiful and she had never seen one so close before. She could feel his breath on her face as he slowly, but gently, stretched his head towards her and, with his long tongue, he gently licked her face. Then, he stood back and lowered his head to Brown Owl, as if he was bowing to her.

"He wants to be friends," whispered Becca, stepping forward and holding out her hand to him. The Stag sniffed Becca's hand, licked it and then stood quietly as Becca carefully ran her hand along his neck. His fur felt velvety to her touch, soft and warm.

"Be careful," warned Brown Owl as the other girls approached the Stag, "don't make any sudden movements which might startle him. Stags can be very dangerous if they feel threatened."

But the Stag didn't seem to the girls to be dangerous as they all stood there stroking him.

He was so beautiful. His coat was reddish-brown in colour and he had white spots over his back. The girls had to stretch up as high as they could to be able to stroke his shoulder.

He blew air from his nostrils in what seemed to be a snort of contentment and then, after a few minutes, he began to back away.

"He's had enough," said Brown Owl, who had been watching him cautiously. She hastily gathering the girls together and bundled them behind her again.

The Stag raised his head, looked down at them
once again as he backed himself into the middle of the

path and then he raised his head to the sky and let out an almighty roar, which made the children jump, before trotting off down the path.

They all watched him as he broke into a trot. As he gathered speed, they all gazed after him until he disappeared into the encroaching darkness of the woodland path.

"Oh, gosh," exclaimed Brown Owl, panting with excitement, "it's getting dark. We'd better hurry and get back to camp before the others send out a search party," and with that, she set off at a fast pace along the path, followed by the girls of Pixies Six who, at that very moment, were probably the happiest girls in the whole world.

By the time they arrived back at the camp the girls were running and they called out to the others who were gathered around the dying embers of the camp fire. The other Brownie leaders had their torches out as it was now dark and the full moon they had seen earlier was rising brightly in the eastern sky.

The other three Sixes had all seen a number of small animals; rabbits; squirrels; butterflies and a variety of birds but none of them had seen the fantastic variety of animals that Pixies Six had seen and fortunately Brown Owl had taken pictures with her mobile phone to show the others just what a wonderful time they had all had.

In the distance they heard the screeching of an Owl as the Brownie leaders passed around mugs of steaming hot chocolate to the now tired girls.

After their hot chocolate, the girls were instructed to go to their tents and collect their wash kits and the Brownie leaders escorted them all to the pavilion to wash and clean their teeth before getting ready to go to bed.

"Thank you, Lily," whispered Becca once again, as she and Emma walked along to the path with their towels and wash bags, "and thank you Cornflower," and, across the clearing and above the roof of the main building, they saw their tiny friends, silhouetted against the full moon as they flew across the night sky.

Chapter Nine

The Visitor In The Night

It was too hot to sleep Becca decided as she lay in her sleeping bag, listening to the steady breathing of her tent mates. The night was still and the gentle rhythmic breathing should have helped her to fall asleep, but she felt restless.

It seemed like hours since they had sipped on their hot chocolate before washing, cleaning their teeth and settling into their tents for the night. The sun seemed to have been out forever and when it finally got dark a full moon rose lighting up the sky once more.

The girls had talked for ages, with their torches switched on so they could see each other. They were all so excited after the nature trail that none of them wanted to go to sleep, or could go to sleep even if they wanted to, so they talked about all the wonderful things they had done that day, such as the nature scavenger hunt, but especially about all the animals they had been so lucky to see on the nature trail and which ones they liked best.

"I liked the grass snake best," said Amy, "I've never seen one before and I always wanted to."

There was a murmur of agreement, and then Emma said, "I liked the deer best. He was so tame.

146

The way he just walked up to us and let us stroke him. And his fur was so soft, just like velvet," she added.

"Me too," said Becca, "that was just so brilliant, it was almost as though he wanted to talk to us."

"Oh, I wish I could talk to the animals," said Lydia.

"Me too," said the other three, all together.

"What about you, Lydia?" said Becca.

"What about me?" Lydia replied.

"What animal did you like best?"

"I liked them all," she replied.

"But if you had to choose one, what would it be?

"Well," she replied, thinking back on all the animals they had seen on the walk, "the owl was brilliant. So were the rabbits, but, if I had to choose one ..."

"You do," Amy interrupted, "we did."

"... then I'd probably go for the badgers. The way those little ones played together and the way that the baby one ran and hid with its mummy, that was so cute."

They all agreed as they remembered the badgers playing together in the woodland clearing.

And so they chattered, on and on, late into the night, until, eventually, the Brownie leaders, checking all was quiet in the camp, had to tell them all to be quiet and that it was time to turn off their torches and go to sleep and, in the darkness of the tent, one by one, the girls drifted into a sleep full of dreams of nature trails and treasure hunts.

Except Becca. Who couldn't get to sleep however hard she tried.

She lay there, snug in her sleeping bag, and stared into the shadows of the tent. She could see the

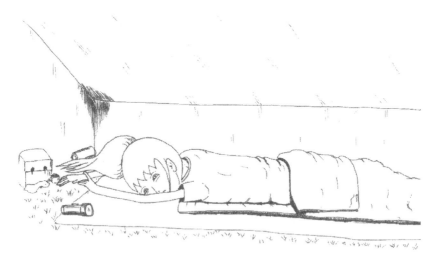

outline of her friends, lying around her, and of their bags and bundles and, gradually, in the darkness her eyelids grew heavy and she began to sink, slowly and peacefully, into the land of nod.

But, just as Becca was on the verge of falling asleep, a loud clap of thunder disturbed the silence of the night and suddenly she was wide awake again.

She sat up and looked around the tent. Her three friends were still fast asleep, their light breathing the only sound in the silent tent.

She wondered if she had really heard the clap of thunder or whether it was all part of a dream she'd dreamed as she was falling asleep.

Had she actually even been asleep? And if so, how long had she been asleep?

She was quite certain that she hadn't been asleep at all, but she didn't have a watch with her so she couldn't check.

As Becca lay there looking at the tent wall she became aware of how bright it was outside. The full moon had risen high in the sky now and, as it was such a clear night, the moon bathed the campsite in a bright silvery light.

It was so hot and Becca carefully unzipped her sleeping bag and, as quietly as she could, she slipped out and lay on top of it.

Because it was dark inside the tent the moon seemed brighter outside.

"Em'?" she whispered to her friend.

There was no reply.

"Em'?" she whispered again, a bit louder this time.

There was a grunt and a rustling as Emma turned over.

"What is it?" came the sleepy reply.

"Are you awake?"

"No," Emma replied.

"Are you sure?"

"Yes."

"It's ever so light outside," said Becca.

In the darkness, she heard Emma sit up. She could see her silhouetted against the wall of the tent and she could see Emma looking around.

"Yes," she said, "it is," and she lay down and turned over to go back to sleep.

"Em'?" whispered Becca.

"Yes?" came the soft reply.

"I can't sleep," Becca told her.

"Nor can I," said Emma with a sigh.

"Why not?"

"Because every time I fall asleep someone wakes me up asking if I'm asleep."

"Was that me?"

"Yes."

"Sorry."

"Close your eyes and count sheep," Emma told her.

"I can't," Becca whispered back, "I can't imagine sheep."

"Well try counting Fairies sliding down a rainbow then," Emma suggested.

"OK, I'll try."

So she lay there, closed her eyes and started counting Fairies sliding down a rainbow. As she did so she could hear the change in Emma's breathing as she fell back to sleep and she crossed her arms crossly and tried to stamp her feet, but when you're lying down trying to get to sleep it really is difficult to stamp your feet, so she glared at the wall of the tent instead, willing the moon to go behind a cloud so she could get to sleep.

She screwed her eyes shut tight, huffed and turned over. Then she couldn't get comfortable so she huffed again and turned over again.

And again.

She opened her eyes and looked at the sides of the tent. The shadow of the branch of a tree waved in the breeze and as she watched it she became aware of a dark shadowy shape creeping along the outside of the tent.

At first it was just a dark shadow, blurry and indistinct. More a growing blob of blackness than any kind of a shape, but as it grew bigger it began to take on a shape.

It appeared to have a long nose and mouth, and large, pointy ears stood up out of the top of its head.

Becca lay watching it, feeling ever so slightly scared.

"Em'?" she whispered.

There was no reply.

"Em'!" she whispered again, digging her friend in the back.

"What is it this time?" Emma said, sounding annoyed to be woken up again.

"Look at the side of the tent."

She heard Emma turn over and gasp.

The shadow of the mouth opened, revealing large, sharp looking teeth.

"What is it?" Emma asked.

"Looks like a crocodile," Becca replied.

"It can't be a crocodile, they don't have long pointy ears."

"I don't know then," said Becca, "perhaps it's a dragon."

"Dragons don't exist," said Emma.

"They might do. We didn't think Fairies existed a few weeks ago, now they are our friends."

"Oh goodness, I do hope it's not a dragon," said Emma, "they breath fire."

"Let's take a look," said Becca, feeling braver now that Emma was awake.

"Let's not," replied Emma and hid under her sleeping bag.

The shadow of the dragon, or whatever creature it was, now had a long neck with triangular spines sticking out along its back.

Becca reached across to Emma and pulled down the top of her sleeping bag.

"Come on Em'," she said, "this could be exciting. Besides I'm sure that Lily and Cornflower wouldn't let anything bad happen to us."

Emma sat up. "But they're not here, are they?" We watched them fly off into the woods and now I'm really scared," and Becca could hear the fear in her friend's voice.

The shadow of the dragon, or whatever creature it was, opened its massive mouth wide and said "ROAR!"

Becca and Emma sat there in silence and looked at each other with puzzled looks on their faces and then burst out laughing.

The roar had been a tiny, high pitched, roar, which had sounded neither loud nor scary and they could hear the sound of two Fairies giggling as the shadow changed from a dragon to those of Lily and Cornflower.

Carefully, and as quietly as they could so as not to wake Lydia or Amy, Becca and Emma crawled across the tent, opened the front flaps, and stood out into the clearing, blinking at the brightness of the moon, which was now a huge, silver disc, high in the night sky.

It was so bright that it cast dark shadows across the clearing and this was how the two Fairies had been able to make their scary dragon show on the side of the tent.

Lily and Cornflower had big grins on their mischievous little faces as Becca and Emma stood up.

"You scared us," said Emma, rather crossly, although she was relieved that there was no dragon.

"What did we look like?" asked Lily.

"A dragon," Emma replied, "and dragons breathe fire and eat people."

"Do dragons really exist?" asked Becca.

"Of course they do," said Lily.

"But they're not allowed out of Fairyland," added Cornflower.

"What're they like?" said Becca, "I mean, really like."

But before the two Fairies could answer a thundering of hooves disturbed the silence of the night.

Startled by the noise, they turned and saw, at the opposite side of the clearing, a beautiful horse of pure white, with a long, flowing mane. It galloped into the clearing of the campsite and skidded to a halt near the campfire and then reared up on its hind legs, kicking its forelegs out in front of it, and whinnied.

The bright moonlight reflected off its sleek white coat and as it reared up Becca and Emma noticed something very strange indeed.

A long, shiny white horn twisted up from the centre of its forehead, shining brightly in the light of the full moon.

It wasn't a horse at all.

"Oh, my goodness," whispered Becca, scarcely able to believe her own eyes, "it's a ..."

"Unicorn," said Emma, overcome with excitement at seeing the mythical creature.

156

"Golly," said Becca, turning to Emma, "are we dreaming?"

"I hope I'm not," came the reply from her friend, "I do so want this to be real."

"I wonder if it is friendly."

"It's so beautiful."

The Unicorn stood still at the far side of the clearing, with its head high, proud and beautiful, staring at the two girls. Then it lowered its head and shook it, its mane flaying wildly about it, loudly snorting as it did so.

The clearing was still and the night was silent. There was no breeze to blow through the leaves, and no sounds could be heard from any woodland creature. For a moment it seemed that the whole world was still, focussed on just them and the Unicorn.

And Lily and Cornflower, who broke the silence with their excited chatter.

"Yes, it is a Unicorn," exclaimed Lily, dancing in front of them.

"No, you're not dreaming," continued Cornflower.

"Yes, it is friendly," added Lily.

"And yes, it is really beautiful," concluded Cornflower, and then added, "but it shouldn't be here."

"Why not?" asked Emma.

"Because, like dragons, they are not allowed out of Fairyland," said Lily.

"So, what's it doing here then?" asked Emma as she and Becca started walking across the clearing followed by the Fairies.

The Unicorn watched them with wide eyes, and gently pawed the ground with its front hoof as it continued to shake its head up and down. It seemed to the girls that the Unicorn was nervous. Well it can't be because of us, thought Becca, we're only little.

As they approached the Unicorn it turned away and, with a loud whinny, it leapt forward and galloped off into the shadows of the woodland path.

The girls stood still, not wanting to frighten the Unicorn away, but wanting so much to run their hands through its flowing mane.

As they stopped, the Unicorn stopped.

It turned its head towards them, raised its head and then whinnied again.

"I think it wants us to follow it," whispered Becca, excitedly, and taking Emma's hand she started off towards the magnificent creature.

"What if it's dangerous?" whispered Emma, pulling back. "What if it is luring us into the woods and into danger?"

Emma was a little frightened at going into the woods at night. In the dark everything looks different, and for a child with imagination, every shadow can look like a dragon, or a goblin, or a monster, each intent on eating little girls who had wandered into the woods after dark. Emma was one of those girls who didn't like to get out of bed in the night in case there were monsters under her bed, ready to grab her feet and take her away to monster land.

"Come on," said Becca, "Lily and Cornflower wouldn't let anything bad happen to us. Would you?"

"No," said Lily and Cornflower together, "but we're not really sure why the Unicorn is here. They usually stay in our world, rarely in yours."

"But they do come to our world sometimes," said Becca, "there's loads of stories about them, so they have been seen before."

"Yes," admitted Lily, "but it is unusual."

So they set off after it, and the Unicorn once again turned away and galloped off along the woodland path.

As they entered the woods and left the bright clearing of the campsite, they stopped for a moment. The girls felt like they were entering a different world.

Ahead of them, through the black, inky darkness, shafts of moonlight shone down through the canopy of branches and leaves above them and in the silence of the surrounding trees they could clearly hear the 'thump-thump' of the Unicorn's hooves as it galloped away before them.

Emma shivered. Not from the cold as it was a warm night, but from her own fear of the dark. She was scared walking through the dark woods but she felt safe as her hand firmly held Becca's.

Their eyes quite quickly adjusted to the darkness of the woods and, accompanied by Lily and Cornflower, Becca and Emma were soon running after the Unicorn to keep up with it. As they ran they held each other's hand to give each other comfort in the earie darkness.

A sudden movement just ahead of them, to their left, made them jump and Emma let out a little gasp of fright, and they stopped.

A paper bag, discarded by a careless and thoughtless Brownie, blew across the path on a sudden slight breeze, its scraping and rustling seeming loud in the silence of the otherwise still night and it cast a long dark shadow as it blew through two shafts of bright moonlight.

Becca and Emma were sure that the pounding of their hearts was so loud that it would wake up the entire camp, but there was no sound of stirring from any of the tents behind them and they relaxed slightly.

A whinny from far ahead of them reminded them that they were meant to be following the

Unicorn and they ran ahead again, hoping they hadn't lost it.

The path turned and twisted ahead of them and the girls began to worry that they might get lost.

"Don't worry," said Lily, flying beside them, "it may be a windy path but it's the same one you started off on, so you'll easily find your camp again."

"And anyway," added Cornflower, "we wouldn't let you get lost."

As soon as Cornflower had spoken the path came to a junction which led either left or right and the Unicorn stood at the junction, waiting for them to catch up.

Once it saw them again, it galloped off along the right path and the girls, followed by Lily and Cornflower, set off eagerly after it.

"It's waiting for us," Becca panted, as she and Emma chased after it, "it wants us to follow it."

"Let's not lose it then," Emma puffed back, running alongside her friend.

"Don't worry," said Lily, flying alongside with Cornflower close behind her, "if he wants to lose us he will. For some reason, he wants us to follow him."

"Why?" asked Emma.

"We don't know," replied Cornflower, "we think he may need your help but we don't know why."

"Our help!" Becca exclaimed. "How does he need our help? What can we do?"

"We don't know," Cornflower replied, "we'll just have to wait and see."

And with that the two Fairies flew on ahead.

Chapter Ten

The Hatchling

The moonlight lit their way along the woodland path as Becca and Emma ran as fast as they could, curious as to why the Unicorn wanted them to follow it. Already they were out of breath, but they didn't give up.

The Unicorn, which stayed ahead of them but never went so far ahead that the girls thought they had lost him, reared up as they rounded the next bend in the woodland path and quickly set off again.

"It's almost as though it's trying to make us hurry," puffed Becca as she ran ahead.

"Yes," Emma panted, trying to keep up with her friend, "it seems quite insistent."

"We've not seen anything like it before," admitted Lily and she flew alongside the girls.

They watched the Unicorn galloping ahead of them and then, suddenly, about fifty metres ahead of them, it veered off the path.

As Becca, Emma and the two Fairies reached the point on the path that the Unicorn had left it, they found a clearing in the woodland and, without hesitation, ran into it.

They were in a large field.

In the middle of the field stood the Unicorn, looking magnificent bathed in the moonlight, its white coat was shiny with sweat and its mane flowed wildly over its neck.

Becca's and Emma's attention were so drawn to the Unicorn that they didn't notice that there was someone else in the field, someone human. The two girls stopped.

She, for it was unmistakably a woman, was kneeling down in the grass with her back to them next to the Unicorn. The Unicorn seemed huge as it stood next to her, pawing the ground.

It whinnied and the woman said something to it that the girls couldn't hear and he seemed to calm down. Then she said, "I was beginning to worry that you two wouldn't get here."

Becca and Emma gasped. They recognised the woman's voice.

"Well," said Barn Owl, standing up and turning towards the girls with a big, friendly smile on her face, "are you going to stand there gawping all night or are you going to help me?"

The two girls stood there, scarcely able to believe their eyes.

"Come on," Barn Owl said, "there's no time to loose, I need your help."

"Come on," urged Lily, "let's go."

Lily and Cornflower both flew towards Barn Owl as Becca and Emma just stood there."

"Don't just stand there," said Barn Owl, "come and help me."

"But we don't know what you want us to do," said Becca as she ran forward, pulling Emma with her.

The Unicorn towered above them as they stood beside it, in front of Barn Owl. They looked up at it, ever so slightly afraid, but the urgency in Barn Owl's voice kept their attention.

On the ground, lying in the long grass, bathed in the bright, white moonlight, lay a huge egg.

They had never seen anything like it before, even the dinosaur egg they saw in the museum when they went to London on a school trip seemed tiny compared to this.

It was the size of a small table, about one metre long and one metre high at its highest point.

And, of course, it was egg shaped. It was rolling around, back and forth, on the ground, and a loud tapping noise was coming from inside of it.

"Right," said Barn Owl, as the two girls ran over to join her, "I need you to help me. Rebecca and Lily, stand over there at one end of the egg and Emma and Cornflower, you stand over there at the other end."

The girls and the Fairies did what Barn Owl told them to do and stood either end of the massive egg. It was nearly as high as them.

"This Unicorn egg," explained Barn Owl, "is due to hatch, but it's having problems because, for some strange reason, it has fallen into our world and in our world the shell is too thick for the hatchling to break it open and hatch, so we need to help it."

"How do we do that?" Emma asked.

"I need you girls to hold each end of the egg as firmly as you can to keep it from rolling about so much. Whatever happens I need you to keep holding it.

"Can you do that?"

Becca and Emma looked at each other and they nodded uncertainly.

"Yes," said Emma, with a certain amount of hesitation, "we think we can."

Lily and Cornflower flew up and said, "we'll try."

"You must be sure," said Barn Owl, "either you can or you cannot. Which is it?"

They were all silent for a moment and then Cornflower said, "Yes. Yes, we can."

"Good," said Barn Owl, "let's get on."

There was an urgent whinnying from the Unicorn and he stamped the ground with his front hooves.

"Yes, yes, I know," said Barn Owl, "we do need to be quick," and she walked around the egg, running her hand over the thick shell as she did so.

"Right girls, now take firm hold your end of the egg and stop it from rolling."

Barn Owl watched as the two girls, assisted by the two Fairies, took firm hold of either end of the huge egg. It was a struggle to hold it as it was frantically moving about and it was really heavy. As they held it they could feel movement from inside the shell. The movement seemed quite urgent, as though the hatchling was desperate to get out but gradually the movement of the egg slowed and Barn Owl bent down and picked up an enormous steel hammer.

She stood up in front of the egg and, again, ran her hand gently over the top of the shell, occasionally tapping it with her knuckles and whispering to it. The moving inside finally stopped completely and, with a grunt of effort, Barn Owl lifted the heavy hammer high above her head and, with a swift movement, brought it crashing down on top of the giant Unicorn egg, about half way between either end.

There was a resounding 'Thud!' as the hammer hit the egg with enormous force and the children felt their arms jarred from the force of the impact.

The Unicorn reared up in front of them and whinnied in alarm at what Barn Owl had done.

And then there was silence.

Somewhere deep within the woods an owl hooted, breaking the silence in the clearing.

Another replied.

The moon had risen higher in the sky and was now right above them.

Becca and Emma were still holding their end of the egg, although Lily and Cornflower had flown into the air, thrown by the impact of the hammer as it hit the shell.

For a moment, nothing happened.

They all held their breath in anticipation.

Then, after what seemed ages, there was a muffled crunching noise and they saw a shadow, which gradually became a thin line, appear across the top of the egg.

Slowly the line grew in length and, inch by inch, it widened, as it enveloped the egg. Then, at the point where Barn Owl's hammer had hit it, a tiny hole appeared.

The line, which was really a crack in the shell, zig-zagged around the egg and they heard the tapping noise from inside begin again.

'Tap-tap, tap-tap' came the noise.

Then silence.

Then it started again after a few moments.

'Tap-tap, tap-tap'.

Then silence again.

This went on for several minutes as they all held their breath in anticipation. The crack in the egg was slowly, but definitely, getting bigger until, at last, a piece of the shell suddenly flew up into the air, landing at Becca's feet and a small horn was sticking out through the shell from the inside.

Almost immediately, the horn disappeared back inside the shell and then, seconds later, a second, larger piece of shell flew into the air and landed on the ground a few feet away.

This time the crack in the shell widened even more until, with a loud 'cracking' noise, the egg bust apart and there before them lay a tiny, baby Unicorn.

"Now girls, move slowly and quietly away," Barn Owl whispered, and without hesitation Becca and Emma stood up and backed away, unable to take their eyes away from the beautiful little Hatchling, lying exhausted on the ground.

As they stood back the Unicorn moved forward and started to gently lick the little Hatchling. Barn Owl stood between Becca and Emma and put her hands on their shoulders. Lily and Cornflower hovered in front of them.

"Well done, girls," said Barn Owl, "you've just helped save its life. If it had been in that shell for just another few minutes it would surely have died."

"But how did it get there?" Becca asked, still watching the little Hatchling as it raised its head up and the Unicorn licked it.

"It was rather unusual," said Sienna, flying out from behind the Unicorn, "it shouldn't have happened."

"What shouldn't have happened," Becca replied, eager to know.

Emma cautiously tiptoed over to the Unicorn as it stood over the Hatchling.

"The doorway between your world and Fairyland is carefully controlled by Pixies," said Sienna, "and usually the door is only opened when it rains and we can come down the rainbow slide.

"Every so often," she continued, "the wind blows the door open for no reason, but normally that doesn't matter because the Pixies simply shut it again and all you might hear is a sound like thunder."

"I thought I heard thunder," Becca said, "I think it woke me up."

"Tonight, something strange happened. This little Hatchling was busy trying to hatch when it rolled out of its nest and fell through the door as it opened and landed here in this field.

"Oh, poor thing," said Emma, who was gently stroking the Unicorn. "It was jolly lucky that the shell didn't break when it landed."

"It's a pity it didn't," said Sienna, "because in your world the shell is much stronger than it is in ours so the Hatchling cannot break the shell by itself."

"Which is why," interrupted Barn Owl, "I had to hit it with my hammer, which was in the toolbox in my car. I had to help to break the shell and let it out, which I managed to do thanks to your help in keeping the egg still."

The girls had forgotten Barn Owl was with them and they both turned to look at her with a puzzled look on their faces.

Barn Owl laughed.

"Don't think you are the only two people in the whole world who can see Fairies, my dears," she said, with a big smile on her face, "Sienna and I have been friends ever since I was a little girl of your age.

"And yes, I knew about your friendship with Lily and Cornflower.

"You are two very lucky little girls."

Becca and Emma blushed and smiled shyly.

"Now," said Barn Owl, "it's the middle of the night and you two should be asleep in your tent and resting for a busy morning tomorrow.

"Let's get back to camp."

The two girls suddenly felt quite sleepy.

"Ooh, I could curl up right here and go to sleep," said Becca, yawning wearily.

"Me too," said Emma, and stretched her arms above her, and shivered.

"Come along then," said Barn Owl, "it's quite a long walk back."

"Awww," said Becca, "I don't think I could walk another step."

She really was feeling tired now. It had been an exciting and busy day and now it had been an exciting and busy night too."

"Come on, Becca," said Emma, taking her hand, "we can make it, I know we can."

"Wait," said Sienna, "I'm sure the Unicorn can give you a ride."

"But what about its little baby?" said Emma.

"Don't worry," came the reply, "it can walk now. Look."

As she spoke the Hatchling struggled to its feet and took a few wobbly steps towards them. It seemed to them to be all long legs and tiny body and it was so wobbly they were sure it was going to fall over.

"We'd better walk back ourselves," said Becca, watching the Hatchling struggling to stay upright on its four wobbly legs, "I don't think he'll make it back to camp.

But as they watched, the Hatchling's step became steadier until, within just a few minutes, it was trotting around the Unicorn as if it had been walking for many years.

"Wow," said Emma, "it learned to walk ever so quickly."

"They do," said Lily, "like us. We can fly within minutes of hatching."

"Gosh, it takes human babies years to walk."

"Yes," said Cornflower, "well usually about a year, but it's still ever so long."

The Unicorn walked towards the girls and knelt down on its front knees, then tucked in its hind legs so it was sitting upright in front of them.

"Climb up on its back," Sienna instructed them, and with the help of Barn Owl, Becca and Emma were soon sitting on the Unicorn's back and he effortlessly stood up, the two girls being no weight to him at all.

They were jolly high, and Becca grasped hold of the Unicorn's thick mane as she felt Emma's arms clasp tightly around her waist.

The early morning sun was already rising in the eastern sky as they entered the clearing where their tents were pitched. Barn Owl and the Hatchling walked along beside them and the Fairies flew with them.

Barn Owl helped the two exhausted girls down from the Unicorn's back and the Unicorn turned and muzzled them. They cuddled it back until they felt Barn Owl pulling them away.

The Unicorn turned and, with a loud 'neigh' it set off at a canter across the campsite, followed closely by the Hatchling.

As they reached the far end of the clearing the girls let out a gasp as they watched a rainbow burst through the sky, flash across the early dawn sky and land just in front of the Unicorn and its Hatchling.

As the Unicorns' galloped into the rainbow they took off and flew up into the air, higher and higher up the rainbow until they disappeared, and with their disappearance, the rainbow disappeared with them.

"Gosh," said Emma.

"Golly," said Becca, as they watched the spectacle before them.

The clearing was silent as the girls ran to their tent, watched by Barn Owl.

They slid quietly into their tent so as not to disturb Lydia and Amy, and climbed wearily into their sleeping bags.

Within a few seconds they were both fast asleep.

Barn Owl smiled and looked at Sienna.

"They are two lucky girls to see a Unicorn," she said and, bidding the Fairies goodnight, she went into her own tent where she, too, was soon asleep.

Chapter Eleven

Fun Activity

The campsite was already a hive of activity when Becca and Emma woke up on Sunday morning. Lydia and Amy were just returning from washing as the two girls stretched and yawned.

"Wake up, you two sleepy heads," said Amy, throwing her washing bag onto her sleeping bag.

"You'll miss breakfast if you don't hurry," said Lydia as she started getting herself dressed.

In a flash Becca and Emma jumped out of their sleeping bags, grabbed their washing bags and ran across the campsite to the pavilion to get washed. Nothing was going to make them miss breakfast, they were both hungry and, as they ran across the field, Becca's tummy started making grumbling noises.

"Let's be quick," she said, "I'm starving."

"Me too," Emma replied.

The pack leaders had cooked bacon, sausages, scrambled eggs and toast and the two girls, hungry from their night activities with Lily, Cornflower and the Unicorn, eagerly stood in the queue for breakfast with the rest of the pack.

Barn Owl winked at them and, with her big friendly smile, gave them each an extra slice of toast.

After breakfast, the pack leaders told the girls to pack up their bags and, once that was done, Barn Owl and Tawny Owl instructed them all in how to let down and fold away the tents, collect up the tent pegs and roll up the ground sheets tidily so that they could be stored away for next time.

It took them about an hour to pack everything away.

"Phew," said Lydia, "it's jolly hot."

The sun was already high in the sky, even though it was quite early in the morning, and there was very little breeze to cool them down.

"We've still got the 'Fun Activity' yet," said Emma.

"Which means," said Amy, "that we'll get even hotter."

Lydia groaned. She didn't like being too hot but, before she could moan about the heat the pack leaders were calling them all to order again.

The girls ran over to where the pack leaders were waiting and quickly lined up in their Sixes.

They were all excited and noisy, as they chatted loudly amongst themselves, each wondering what the 'Fun Activity' was going to be.

Brown Owl raised both of her hands and placed them on top of her head. This was a sign that she wanted the girls to stop chattering and pay attention to what she had to say.

It worked and in no time the girls had fallen silent and were looking expectantly at Brown Owl.

For a moment all they could hear was the chirping and tweeting of the birds in the trees surrounding the campsite. The birds' tweeting was loud as Blackbirds competed with Sparrows and Thrushes to be the loudest and the Wren, the smallest bird of all, shouted aggressively at all of them.

"Right girls," said Brown Owl, once she had their attention, "I hope you all had a wonderful day yesterday."

All the girls cheered as Brown Owl looked at the sea of happy faces as they all remembered the nature scavenger hunt, the twilight nature trail and the songs and activities around the campfire, including the rescue of the little hedgehog.

"Today we have just one activity and then this year's Pack Holiday Weekend will be over," and here all the girls groaned, and some even booed, "and your Mummies and Daddies will be here to pick you up and take you home.

"I must say, and I think I speak for all the pack leaders, that you have all been wonderful, you have all worked hard and you have all behaved as we would expect a Brownie to behave. Well done to all of you and let's give yourselves a clap."

The girls clapped and cheered and jumped about as they glowed with pride at Brown Owl's praise.

"Can I remind you all," Brown Owl continued when the girls had calmed down again, "that you are not to leave the camp to go home without first telling your pack leader and signing out. This is so we know that you have been safely collected, and if you are going home with someone else's Mummy and Daddy, we should already have been told.

"So, Sprites will tell Barn Owl, Gnomes, you are tell Tawny Owl, Elves, Snowy Owl is your pack leader, and Pixies, you are to come to me. Is that clear?"

Brown Owl looked at the smiling faces of the girls standing in front of her, all nodding to show that they understood what she had said, and she smiled.

"Right," she said, "this morning is called Fun Activity and there are three points to be won by the winning Six and then we'll be able to announce the winning Six for the whole weekend. Tawny Owl, will you please let the girls know what points each Six currently has?"

Tawny Owl stepped forward and unfolded a piece of paper.

"At the moment, Pixies Six is in the lead with twelve points," Becca, Emma, Lydia and Amy all jumped around Freya and Beth in their excitement, "close behind them, on eleven points are Elves, and Sprites and Gnomes you are joint third place with ten points each. This means that any Six can win the weekend by winning this morning's Fun Activity."

As Tawny Owl folded her piece of paper and put it back into her pocket a tiny voice whispered in Becca's ear.

"What is the fun activity?"

"Shh," Becca replied, as quiet as possible so no one would look at her, "Brown Owl is just about to tell us."

Brown Owl stepped forward again. "Now, you're probably wondering what the fun activity is going to be," she said, as if she had heard Becca's reply to Lily, and all the girls shouted "Yes" in reply.

"Well," she continued, looking at the sea of expectant faces in front of her and smiling, "in a minute," she was clearly going to keep the girls in suspense for a while longer, "we'll be taking all of our bags and things to the main pavilion and we'll meet our instructors for the morning, who will tell us all about it."

Instructors?

There was a hubbub of noise as the girls started chatting excitedly amongst themselves, wondering what activity was lined up for them.

"Now, everyone, please collect your bags and follow your Pack Leader to the pavilion, and girls, please make sure you don't leave anything and we won't be coming back here afterwards."

There was a collective groan from the girls as the all wanted to know what the fun activity was going to be.

As quick as they could they all ran to where their tents had been and collected their bags. They had already picked up all the litter and rubbish and the dustbin bags were piled up in the centre of the field. The tents, pegs and groundsheets would be collected by the people who ran the Florence Walker Memorial Centre.

"Can we join in?" asked Lily as they walked along the woodland path towards the pavilion building.

"We don't even know what we're doing yet," said Becca.

"Never mind," Lily replied, "we like surprises, don't we Cornflower?"

"Ooh yes," Cornflower replied, "I'm so looking forward to what it is you're going to do."

"Me too," said Emma, "I just hope we like it."

They were silent for a moment and then Emma said, "How come you didn't tell us that Brown Owl was a friend of yours?"

"She isn't," said Cornflower.

"But you know her," Emma insisted.

"Oh yes, she's a friend of Sienna's. Sienna first came to Bluebell Wood when Brown Owl was a little girl of about your age."

"Golly," said Emma, "as long ago as that?"

"It was only about twenty years ago," said Lily.

"Wow, Brown Owl must be ever so old."

"Probably about the same age as your Mummy," said Lily, laughing.

"Exactly," said Becca.

They arrived at the main pavilion and piled their bags in a room that was then locked up. Then the Pack Leaders lead them out through a back door and into a large field at the back of the pavilion.

In the field stood four, very high, frames. They were made up of three wooden poles that were joined together at the top. Ropes hung down from a bar near the top and several large stacks of what looked like crates for holding bottles, were in the centre of the field in the middle of the four wooden frames.

The girls looked up at the huge frames with growing excitement, wondering what they would have to do. The frames looked ever so high.

"We're going to be tied to ropes and lifted into the air," said Lydia, nervously.

"I hope not," said Amy, "I really don't like heights."

"Me neither," agreed Lydia.

"Girls," said Brown Owl, clapping her hands together to get their attention, "now please pay attention. This morning's activity is called the Crate Stack Challenge."

All the girls looked at Brown Owl and then at each other with puzzled looks on their faces. None of them knew what the Crate Stack Challenge was.

"The Crate Stack Challenge," said Brown Owl, as if she had read their thoughts, "is simple. The aim of the game is to build a stack of crates and the team that builds the highest stack wins. The end of the game is when all the stacks have fallen and the one that had the most crates in their stack before it fell will be the winner."

Freya put her hand in the air.

"Yes, Freya?" said Brown Owl, and Freya blushed as she became aware that all the other girls were looking at her.

"Please, Brown Owl," she said, "what are these big frames for?"

"I'm glad you asked me that," Brown Owl replied with a smile, "does anyone have any suggestions?"

No one made a sound.

"OK," Brown Owl continued, "let me introduce you to your instructors and judges for this morning's activity," and with that Brown Owl turned around to face the group of six grown-ups who had been standing silently behind her.

The six grown-ups were wearing helmets and blue boiler suits with 'Crate Stack Challenge Team' in big yellow letters on their left breast pocket.

One of the men stepped forward and stood beside Brown Owl.

"Good morning, girls," he said with a friendly smile, "welcome to Crate Stack Challenge. My name is Eddie and my assistants today are Stuart, Jane, Christine, Lynne and Johnny."

As he said each name so the person who's name it was stood forward and waved. The girls waved back. When the introductions were over Eddie continued.

"This game is a lot of fun and very safe as long as you are all sensible and listen to what we tell you." Eddie looked at all the expectant faces in front of him and smiled again.

"He's got a nice smile," said Lily quietly, "but we still don't know what the Crate Stack Challenge is."

"Me neither," said Becca.

"Nor me," added Emma.

They all looked at Cornflower.

"Don't look at me," she said, "I don't know either."

"So, what are you going to do?" asked Eddie.

There was silence.

"Any ideas?"

Someone said. "Stack crates?"

"Yes," said Eddie, "that's exactly what you're going to do, but Brown Owl already told you that much.

"So, the Crate Stack Challenge is going to test your problem-solving skills; your balance; your courage; your building skills and, above all, your ability to work together, what we call your team work skills.

"Two girls from each six will stand on top of the tower of crates as it gets higher and the whole team will have to think of more and more clever ways of getting the crates to the top of the stack without knocking it down. But beware, the higher it gets the wobblier it will get, and, like a tooth that's ready to come out, the more it wobbles, the more likely it is to fall over."

He looked at the girls. He was pleased to see that they were all paying attention to what he was saying.

"Everyone will wear a hard hat, like the one me and my assistants are wearing. This is to protect your head in the unlikely case that a crate should fall and hit you.

"Two girls from each six will be chosen by the six, if you cannot choose then Brown Owl will make the choice for you. These two girls will be the ones who will stand at the top of the stack and place the crates in place when your friends pass a crate up to you.

"The girls at the top will also wear a harness, just like the ones Jane and Lynne are wearing." Everyone looked at the ladies called Jane and Lynne.

"You will have a rope attached to your harness which is firmly attached to each frame using a device called an Auto-Belay, like the one Stuart is holding up for you to see."

Stuart stepped forward and held up a heavy looking blue and white device.

"As you get higher this Auto-Belay," Eddie continued, "will automatically pull in the rope that is attached to the climbers, so that, if you fall, or when your crate stack collapses, you will be lowered slowly and, most importantly, safely to the ground.

"In a moment, my team will demonstrate how to build a stack and then it'll be your turn, but before we start the demonstration, are there any questions?"

One girl put her hand in the air.

"Yes, Georgina?" said Brown Owl.

"Please, Mr Eddie," said Georgina, "Brown Owl said the winning team is the one with the most crates in their stack before it falls?"

"That's right," said Eddie.

"So, it's not the last stack standing that wins then?"

"That is absolutely right, Georgina, no, it isn't. This is not a race to see who can build their stack fastest, but who can build it highest. One of my team will be with each six and will count how many crates high you get before yours falls down."

Another girl put her hand up.

"Yes, Alexandra?"

"Please, Mr Eddie," said Alexandra, "what's the highest stack ever made?"

"Well young lady," said Eddie, "if you are asking about the highest stack I've seen built, then it is 18 crates, is that right Lynne?"

"That's right, Eddie," replied Lynne.

"Which is very high, but if you're asking what is the highest stack ever built anywhere then I don't really know. Probably about 28.

"Any more questions?"

All the girls stood there, looking up at the frames and shaking their heads. Eddie noted that, as often happened when he ran the Crate Stack

Challenge, some girls looked quite excited and some looked very nervous. Going up on a stack of crates was not for everyone and as he looked around he knew which of the girls were going to go up and be at the top of the stack and he knew which ones were not, and he was rarely wrong.

"Right," he said, "we'll do our demonstration and, if everything is clear, we'll get you all set up and we can start the game.

"Now, as we have already said, Jane and Lynne are both wearing a harness which means that they will stand on top of the stack as it gets higher."

Jane and Lynne both walked over to the nearest frame, attached a rope to themselves and stood in the centre of the frame. The other three lined up, Johnny stood by Jane and Lynne, Stuart was by the pile of crates and Christine stood about half way between them.

Eddie explained to the girls that Stuart was going to pass a crate to Christine, who would then pass it to Stuart, who would, in turn, place in on the ground.

"Are you ready?" Everyone nodded and he blew his whistle.

Stuart picked up a crate and, instead of running to Christine as they were expecting, he threw it.

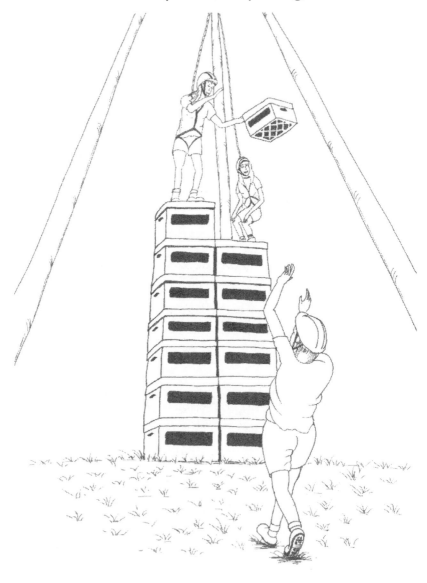

Christine caught it, turned, and threw it to Johnny,

who placed it on the ground next to where Jane was standing. Jane and Lynne stood on the crate as another one flew across the field and was placed next to the first. Johnny placed the third crate on top of the second one and Jane and Lynne stepped up onto it and the fourth and fifth crates to arrive were stacked on top of the first, allowing Jane and Lynne to step up onto the first stack again.

And so it went on, building each stack for Jane and Lynne to step up to until the stack was too high for Johnny to place the next crate on so he passed it to Jane and from then on the two ladies took on the task of building the stack higher and higher.

There were ropes hanging down and Johnny started tying crates to the ropes and Jane and Lynne were able to pull the crates up and continue to build.

As the stack got higher it became more and more wobbly until one of the stacks moved away from the other and started to fall to the ground and, as Jane and Lynne slipped off the top they swung in the air, suspended on their ropes, and knocked the other stack and it too fell.

The team on the ground stepped aside as the two stacks fell so that the crates didn't land on top of them, and the two stacks fell harmlessly, but noisily, to the ground.

For a moment Jane and Lynne seemed to hang in the air, swinging, and then, ever so gently, the Auto-Belay lowered them safely to the ground.

Chapter Twelve

The Crate Stack Challenge

"Right," said Freya, gathering the girls of her six together, "who really doesn't want to go up on the pile of crates?"

Amy, Lydia and Beth all put their hands in the air.

"That just leaves you two," said Freya, looking at Becca and Emma, "are you two happy to build the crate tower and go all that way up?"

Becca looked at Emma. She wanted to go up, but she felt a little bit scared at the thought of being so high. Emma smiled nervously at her and they both looked at Freya.

"Yes," said Becca, deciding to take the plunge and squeezing Emma's hand as she did so.

"Don't be scared," said Lily to the two girls, "it looks jolly good fun."

"And we will help you," added Cornflower, flying around Emma's head.

"How come," Emma whispered to Cornflower, as she flew another circle around Emma's head, "no-one else can see you flying around like that?"

"We're invisible to children who don't believe in Fairies," Cornflower replied, as if Emma should know that.

"But Lydia believes in Fairies," Emma said, "she told us last night."

"We've made ourselves invisible," said Lily, "so she can't see us."

"Oh," said Becca, "isn't that a bit unfair?"

"Oh no," said Lily, "if her belief was strong enough she would be able to see us."

"Just like you did," added Cornflower, "that day we first came into the forest and you saw us. You weren't meant to see us, you know."

"I remember," said Becca, laughing, "we got told off by Sienna."

"And you'll get told off again," said Freya, interrupting them, thinking they were talking to each other, "if you don't stop talking and start paying attention."

"Sorry, Freya," they both said together, trying to keep a straight face as they listened to Lily and Cornflower laughing and twittering knowing jolly well that only Becca and Emma could hear them.

"Right," Freya continued once she was sure everyone was paying attention, "this is how we'll work it. Becca and Emma will be on the stack, Beth and I will pass the crates up to you and Amy and Lydia will bring the crates from the pile.

"When the crate stack is too high for us to pass them up we'll tie them to a rope and haul them up to you."

Freya looked about her to make sure everyone had understood her instructions.

"OK?" she said.

"Yes, Freya," the girls replied.

Once they had decided how they were going to play the challenge Becca and Emma were sent over to the instructors.

"You've been chosen to be at the top of your pile, have you?" said the lady called Jane. She had friendly, pale blue-grey eyes and her lightly tanned face was framed by shoulder length strawberry blond wavy hair.

Her pretty smile helped the two girls relax.

"Let's get you both strapped up then," she said and handed Becca and Emma a blue harness each.

With a little bit of help from Jane, Becca and Emma stepped into their harnesses and pulled it up around their legs. Then they pulled the top straps over their shoulders so they could fasten all the straps into the big clip at the front. It was a bit like fastening the seat belts in Mummy's car.

Jane stood in front of Becca and grabbed her straps, lifting her gently off the ground.

"Does that hurt?" she asked.

"No," said Becca, and Jane lowered her down

and repeated the exercise on Emma, with the same answer.

"Excellent," said Jane, once she'd put Emma down, "your harnesses are both secure and you're ready to climb.

"Now then," she continued, "before you climb I will attach your harness to the rope hanging between that frame," and she pointed to one of the frames near to where the rest of the Pixie Six were standing.

Becca and Emma could see that two girls from each of the other sixes were also wearing harnesses.

"The Auto-Belay, that Eddie told you about, will pull up the rope you'll be attached to. As you get higher the rope will automatically get shorter and, when your crate stack collapses, as it will do, you will be gently lowered to the ground, as you saw earlier when Lynne and I were on the stack."

She smiled at them again, a beaming smile that filled them with confidence.

"Happy?" she said.

"I think so," said Becca, and Emma nodded her head in agreement.

"OK, good," she said, then she stood and shouted out, so everyone could hear, "Pixies Six, ready."

"Elves Six, ready," came the reply, quickly followed by, "Gnomes Six, ready," and "Sprites Six, ready."

"Right," said Eddie, "just remember, this is not about who is the fastest, but about who can build the highest crate stack.

"In our experience, the more you try and rush it the quicker your crate stack will fall over.

"Now, let's play!"

Eddie blew a loud blast on his whistle and with that Becca and Emma ran to the large frame where Jane, carefully, attached them to a large metal clip and buckled it shut. Then, just to be sure, she tested it once again.

"There," she said, crouching down in front of the two girls, "that's nice and secure. Now, remember what Eddie said, don't rush; build your stack carefully and if you take care you'll get higher without it collapsing.

"Good luck," she added, as Freya and Beth placed the first two crates next to each other on the ground at the centre of the frame.

"This is going to be so much fun," said Cornflower, as she and Lily flew in and out of the crates that Freya and Beth had just placed there.

"Come on," said Lily, whizzing past, "get on your create otherwise it'll be too high for you to climb onto."

Quick as a flash the two girls stood on the first crate and watched Lydia and Amy running across the field with the next crates, pass them to Freya and Beth, and run back to the pile for more. Unlike the grown-ups, none of the Brownies were able to throw the crates to one another, so the Brownies were kept running back and forth to bring the crates to their stack.

Freya carefully put the next crate down on top of the first one and Becca and Emma carefully stepped up onto it to allow Beth to place hers beside it.

The crate stack wobbled.

"Oooh," said Emma, "it's already wobbling and there's only two crates in our stack."

"Don't worry, Em," said Becca, "just hold on to me and you'll be OK. We'll get the hang of it in a minute."

While they were waiting for the next crates they took the opportunity to look around to see how the others were doing.

All the other stacks were also just two crates high so far, but then, the game had only just started.

"We think we can get the highest," said Lily, who was still flying in and out of the crates on which Becca and Emma were standing.

"Wee!" said Cornflower, following her sister. As she flew through the crate she accidentally clipped its edge and the crate wobbled.

"Whoa!" said Lily, flying into the air.

"Whoops," said Cornflower, "Sorry."

The next crate was added to the stack, followed quickly by another.

The sun was high, golden and bright in the clear blue sky, and the girls could feel its heat beating down upon them. There was no shade in the field in which they were playing. The two Fairies now sat quietly on Becca's and Emma's shoulders so they would not accidentally cause their crate stack to collapse.

"Do you want us to fly over and knock the other stacks over?" asked Lily.

"Certainly not," Becca replied, "that wouldn't be nice."

"It would be fun though."

"No."

"Alright, we won't."

"We promise," added Cornflower.

In what seemed no time at all the four stacks of crates had grown and soon they were all too high for the girls on the ground to just place the next crate on top of the stack.

With Becca kneeling down on one stack and Emma standing on the second and holding her left arm, Becca reached down with her right hand and hauled the next crate up.

And the stack wobbled.

And began to topple.

"Quick, hold me, Em," Becca cried out and Emma pulled Becca's arm and pulled her back.

But the stack on which Emma was standing also started to wobble.

"I think we're going to fall," she said.

With a flash of blue and green, Lily and Cornflower quickly flew to the crates and steadied them.

"Phew, I thought we were going to fall then," said Emma.

"Me too," Becca replied, then called down to Freya and Beth, who were ready with the next crates, "I don't think leaning down to pull up the crates is such a good idea, we nearly toppled over just then."

"OK," Freya replied, "we'll try tying it to one of these ropes and you'll have to haul it up yourselves."

"How are you girls doing?" asked Jane, striding over to them. She had been watching their progress and had seen their remarkable recovery. "It's going to get quite difficult from here on. How are you planning to get the crates up now?"

Freya explained to Jane how they thought they might use the ropes.

"Excellent idea," Jane exclaimed, and the Pixie Six girls all looked pleased with themselves.

In their Brownie meetings before the school holidays the girls had been learning how to tie knots. Now they had to remember which was the best knot to use and, more importantly, how to tie and untie it. As the crates were quite light they decided to use a Clove Hitch, a knot that is both easy to tie and untie, but one which, the girls decided, would be strong enough to hold the crate as Becca and Emma hauled it up.

With advice and help from the instructors, all four Sixes were soon carefully hauling up crates on their ropes and slowly, but surely, the crate stacks grew higher and higher.

And higher still.

And at eleven crates high the first stack collapsed.

Becca and Emma had both been concentrating so hard on their stack, making sure that they didn't make any sudden movement that would cause it to fall, that they weren't paying attention to any of the other stacks.

In fact, every Brownie playing the game was concentrating on their own stack and had become completely unaware of what was happening with the other stacks until, with a mighty crash, and a squeal from the girls of The Elves Six, the first of the stacks of crates tumbled noisily to the ground and the two Brownies who were on top of the stack were, momentarily, left hanging in the air until their auto-belay lowered them safely to the ground, where they were met by the instructors and released from their harnesses.

"Wow," said Becca to Emma, as they all stopped and watched the crates fall. It was as though they had fallen in slow motion. First of all the crates in the stack all toppled together, as though it was one single tower, all fixed together, then, about half way on its fall the stack seemed to bend and all of the crates above fell loose from the rest and crashed down on the crates below.

When they hit the ground the crates bounced, and those that had been at the top rolled over and over until they came to a higgledy-piggledy halt on the grass.

"Eleven crates," called Eddie. "Well done Elves, that was good for a first attempt.

"Now, girls," he continued, "go and stand with your Leaders and watch the rest of the game."

Disappointed at not getting higher the girls of Elves Six ran across the field to stand with Brown Owl, Barn Owl, Tawny Owl and Snowy Owl.

"Well done, girls," said Brown Owl, "that was a jolly good game. Did you enjoy yourselves?"

Her question was met with enthusiastic replies from the girls of Elves Six, who really had enjoyed the game.

And then there was a second crash.

They all turned in time to see the Sprites Six stack fall to the ground.

"Twelve crates," called Eddie and soon the girls of Sprites Six had joined those of Elves Six with the Brownie leaders.

"How high to you want to go?" asked Lily, as she and Cornflower steadied the crate that Becca and Emma were untying.

The girls carefully placed the crate on top of their stack and climbed up onto it to wait for the next one.

"Oh, I don't know," said Becca, "enough to win, I suppose."

"It's ever so high," said Emma and both girls looked down at the field below them.

The other girls from Pixies Six couldn't reach the top crates anymore, even if they reached up on tiptoe. Even Jane, who was really tall, couldn't reach the top.

"It's funny," said Becca, looking cautiously about her, "how it looks so much higher when you're on top of the stack than it looked when Jane and Lynne were building theirs and we were on the ground."

"And theirs was much higher."

"I do wish it wouldn't wobble so much, though."

With another flash of blue and green, Lily and Cornflower flew round and round the top crates, faster and faster, and the stack stopped wobbling.

"Thanks," said Emma. "What did you do?"

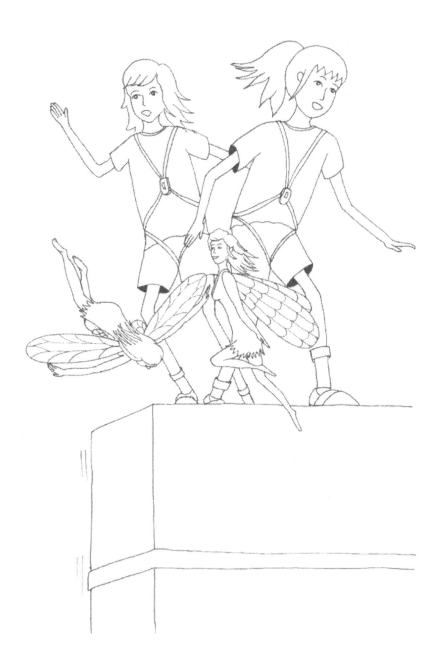

"What you wished for," replied Cornflower, "we've stopped it wobbling."

"Did you use magic?"

"Only a little bit," she replied.

"Isn't that cheating?"

"Possibly," Cornflower said, "but we prefer to think of it as assisting, and what's the point in having Fairies as friends if we're not allowed to assist you?"

"Anyway," Lily added, "it would only be cheating if we helped you win by knocking down the other stacks, and you told us we weren't allowed to do that."

"And," Cornflower continued, "your stack can still fall over, we just stopped it wobbling so much."

Reassured, Becca and Emma untied the next crate and added it to the stack.

Now their stack was steady it was easier to grow it. Soon they were up to fifteen crates in their stack.

"We're about as high as our bedroom window," Becca said, looking down again.

They could see Lydia and Amy running across the field with more crates and Freya and Beth just below them waiting. While they were waiting, Becca and Emma looked at the Gnomes stack. They had fourteen crates already and were busy hauling their next one up.

"Gosh, they're doing well," said Becca. The girls from Elves and Sprites were all cheering them on.

"Come on, Gnomes, the Pixies are beating you," someone shouted.

"Pixies 15; Gnomes 14," someone else sang out and the girls all started chanting; "fifteen, fifteen, one more; one more."

As if the chanting had given them a challenge, the girls on top of the Gnomes' stack gave a sudden tug on the rope they were using to pull up the crate, which caused it to start swinging.

The crate swung away from the stack.

Silence fell as all the girls, all the Brownie Pack leaders and all the instructors held their breath and watched the crate as it swung out in a circle, away, then around; and then it was swinging back towards the stack of crates.

For one moment, it looked as though the swinging crate was going to collide with the stack but luckily it swung harmlessly past, missing the stack by just a few centimetres.

There was a huge, loud, sigh of relief from all the watchers. Even Becca and Emma had been holding their breath. A few of the girls started clapping as the stack looked safe and, just as they were turning to each other to talk about how close the crate had been to the stack, it swung in once again and this time collided with the stack full on about three quarters of the way to the top.

It hit the stack square in the middle and bounced back.

The stack wobbled and collided with the next stack.

The tops of the two stacks moved apart as the crate on the end of the rope swung back in, hitting the first stack for a second time.

Caught off balance, the crate knocked the stack one way as the girls who were standing on top trying to keep their balance, were still going the other way.

The first stack once again collided with the second stack and this time it went out further and, slowly, slowly, it started to topple.

The girls fell off the top of the stack on which they had been standing and were, suddenly, handing in mid-air as the crate stacks fell crashing to the ground below them.

Then, after a short moment, they were lowered gently and safely to the ground where Lynne and Christine were, once again, there to unclip them after they had landed.

"Fourteen crates," shouted Eddie, "well done, Gnomes Six, a very good effort.

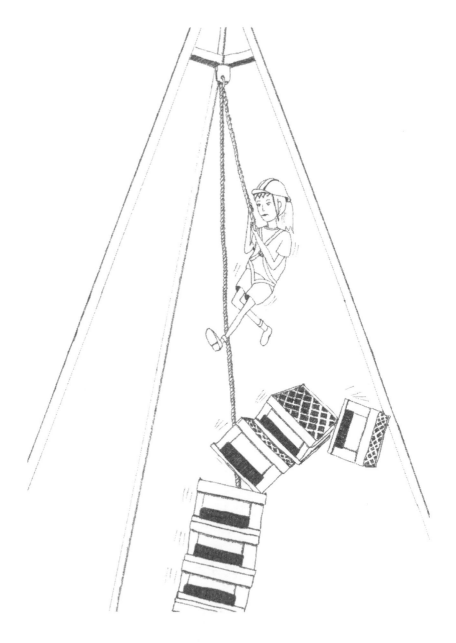

"That means," he continued, "that Pixie Six is the winner as they already have fifteen crates in their stack."

All the girls were cheering as the stack beneath Becca and Emma suddenly collapsed, the Fairy Magic that had been holding them steady suddenly wasn't holding them anymore.

"Wee," said Lily, "enjoy the drop."

It seemed to both girls that they were dangling high above the field for ages before the auto-belay began lowering them towards the ground.

"Wow, this is fun," shouted Emma and she threw out her arms, pretending she was flying through the air, just like a Fairy.

Chapter Thirteen

The End of Camp

It all seemed to happen so fast.

One minute Becca was standing on a stack of fifteen crates piled up, each on top of the other and hauling up the next crate which was tied to the end of the rope.

She even had time to look around her. A sea of faces looked up at her, all her friends from Elves, Sprites and Gnomes Sixes.

She could see the Pack leaders, smiling up at her.

Lily and Cornflower were flying around her and Emma, unseen by all the other girls.

And the view of the campsite was fantastic.

Then there was a blur as she dropped suddenly and very fast for several metres.

She heard a loud gasp from her friends.

And then, with a bone shaking jolt, she stopped.

Because she had fallen so far so fast, when she stopped she bounced back up and Becca rose up once more.

And then she stopped going up.

And she dropped again.

And stopped.

And then she wasn't falling any more.

In fact, she wasn't moving at all.

She was just hanging there, half way between the top of the frame and the ground.

She spun around, first one way, then the other way, then back again, until, eventually, she stopped and hung there.

She became aware of the instructors running across the field to below where she was hanging and she could hear the Pack leaders calling all the other girls to them, to get them out of the way.

One of the girls screamed, "what if she falls? She might die!"

Becca heard Barn Owl telling the girl to 'shush'."

Brown Owl called up, "Rebecca, are you all right?"

"I-I think so, Brown Owl, is Emma alright?"

"Don't worry, dear, Emma landed safely. The instructors will get you down, just don't be frightened."

"I'm not frightened, Brown Owl," Becca replied, but both of them knew that that wasn't true. Becca was very scared and Brown Owl was very worried about Becca.

Becca held on to the rope and looked down.

She was still a long way up in the air; higher, it seemed, than when she was on top of the stack, but that was only because she was in danger of falling.

She could see Emma clinging to Brown Owl, hiding her face in her shoulder.

"I'm OK, Em'," she called down to her friend.

Emma looked up.

"Do be careful, Becca," she called back.

Becca became aware of Lily and Cornflower flying beneath her. They were flying round and round in a tight circle, spinning faster and faster.

She saw Jane grab hold of one of the ropes and start climbing up it towards her.

And then there was Sienna.

"Don't worry, Rebecca," said Sienna, "Lily and Cornflower are spinning below you, creating a cushion of air beneath you, which is stopping you from falling.

"In a few seconds, they'll lower you to the ground.

"Just hold on tightly to the rope and keep yourself upright and you've got nothing to worry about."

"Am I flying?" Becca asked.

"In a way, yes, you are," Sienna replied, "with the help of Lily and Cornflower."

It was as if she could feel the cushion of air that Lily and Cornflower were creating for her, as they began to lower her, slowly and steadily, towards the ground.

Everything was happening in slow motion.

Other Fairies had joined Lily and Cornflower and she could hear them singing.

"That's right," said Sienna, when Becca asked her if it really was singing she could hear, "that's a flying spell they're singing, it's what's keeping you from falling and hurting yourself."

Before Becca could ask any more questions about the flying spell, Sienna continued, "it's a very difficult spell. It takes all their energy and concentration. So much that they won't be able to fly away when they land you."

"Oh, no," wailed Becca, "what will happen to them? Will they be alright? They won't die, will they?"

"Look around you, Becca," said Sienna, and Becca realised that she had her eyes shut tight. She opened them and looked down.

She saw a blur of colour, red, yellow, orange, below her and she could suddenly see other Fairies flying towards them.

"When you are safely down, these Fairies will take Lily, Cornflower and the other Fairies who are holding you up, and take them away to rest. It will be a few days until they are fully recovered."

"Will they be alright though?"

"Oh yes, it's just that you humans are so heavy that it takes a lot of magic to keep you in the air, it's not something that Fairies are normally able to do. At least for very long. Lily and Cornflower will be especially exhausted as they were on their own for quite a while before they were joined by Rose and Petunia."

"You're being ever so brave," said Jane, who had climbed the rope and had reached Becca "and it looks as though the auto-belay has started working again."

Becca felt hands holding her as she was lowered to the ground and unhooked from the rope.

Brown Owl scooped her up and carried her away.

"Are you alright, Rebecca?" she asked as she put her down. Emma ran across and hugged her.

"Oh, I was so scared," said Emma, holding her friend tightly, "I thought you were hurt the way you bounced on the end of that rope."

"I'm alright, Em', I promise," said Becca, comforting her friend, "the bouncing did hurt a bit, but not too badly."

Barn Owl, walked across to them and knelt in front of the girls. She lowered her voice to a whisper, "Thank goodness," she said, "for our Fairy friends. Without them you might have fallen and broken a leg, or something."

"How about Lily and Cornflower and the others?" asked Becca.

"Oh, they'll be alright," Barn Owl replied, "they've already been carried away by their friends. You'll see them again in a couple of days, when they've recovered."

"I didn't thank them," said Becca.

"There'll be plenty of time for that," came the reply, "now, if you're feeling alright, you can go and join your Six."

Becca and Emma ran over to Freya, Beth, Lydia and Amy.

"Are you alright, Becca?" said Freya, as the other girls gathered around Becca and Emma. They all started speaking at once and Becca assured them all that she was a bit shaken, but otherwise, just fine.

"I would have been so scared," said Emma, "I know I would."

"I was scared, Em'," Becca replied, "but Lily and Cornflower were helping me and they would never let me get hurt."

"Do you think you were in any danger?"

"I don't know, but Lily and Cornflower were using magic to bring me to the ground. A lot of magic, according to Sienna."

They became aware that the Pack Leaders were, once again, calling them to gather around Brown Owl and pay attention. All the girls, obediently ran in and fell silent, waiting for Brown Owl to speak.

"First," said Brown Owl, "thanks to the quick action of our instructors, I am pleased to say that we managed to avoid an accident just now when Becca's rope got stuck. Fortunately, she wasn't in any serious danger, but I'm sure we all held our breath for a few moments while she was stuck up there."

All the girls started talking at once, as they agreed that they had, in fact, been holding their breath for minutes, and they all wanted Becca to tell them what had happened.

"Girls," said Brown Owl, loudly, "girls! I didn't say you could all start talking, now did I?"

The girls became silent.

"That's better," said Brown Owl, looking at each of the girls standing in front of her.

"It wasn't the instructors who saved you," Emma whispered to Becca, "it was Lily and Cornflower."

"I know, and so does Barn Owl," Becca replied, "but she can hardly tell Brown Owl that I was saved by a couple of Fairies, can she?"

"I suppose not," Emma replied.

"….. and I'm pleased to say," they were suddenly aware that Tawny Owl was talking, "that Pixies Six are the winners of this year's Camp Challenge. Well done girls, and well done everyone for taking part."

Becca, Emma and the girls from Pixies Six all jumped up and down with joy, hugging each other, and squealing with excitement. This was the first camp Becca and Emma had ever been on and they were so excited to win the Camp Challenge with their Six.

"And now," Brown Owl continued when the girls had quietened down a bit, "can the Pixies Sixer come up and collect the Camp Challenge Cup."

Freya proudly walked up to Brown Owl and stood before her. She stood to attention and gave Brown Owl the Brownie salute. Brown Owl saluted back, presented Freya with a beautiful, shiny silver cup, and shook her hand in congratulation.

"Well done, Freya, and well done all Brownies for an exemplary weekend. I know that all of your Brownie Leaders who have worked so hard, have also had a wonderful weekend, so let's give them a big Brownie 'thank you'."

There were cheers as the girls started clapping to show their appreciation for the Brownie Leaders.

"We also hope that you have enjoyed your weekend as much as we have."

Another cheer and more clapping from the girls.

"And finally, before we finish up here, I want everyone to show their appreciation for our instructors this morning who have, I'm sure you'll agree, given us a wonderful and fun game, with the Crate Stack Challenge."

As the girls cheered and clapped, the instructors stopped what they were doing, momentarily, and waved at the girls.

* * * * *

They were all gathered around Eddie, who was inspecting the Auto Belay that had failed.

"I don't know how it stopped that little girl from falling," he said, "it's clearly faulty."

"She was lucky," said Lynne,

"Yes, she could have been hurt," added Jane.

"We'll have to fill in an accident report, and we'll have to have a full Health and Safety inspection before we can do another demonstration.

"We'll test every Auto Belay we've got in stock," Eddie continued. "I've never known one to fail before, they just shouldn't.

He was turning the Auto Belay over in his hand, studying it closely. As he did so he noticed something that didn't seem quite right to him.

He looked even closer, then turned to Johnny. "Have you got a small, flathead screwdriver on you, Johnny?"

Johnny patted his pockets and produced a small screwdriver.

"Here," he said.

Eddie turned the Auto Belay towards him, carefully inserted the screwdriver and then turned the Auto Belay over again. A tiny pebble dropped out into the palm of his hand. As he withdrew the screwdriver there was a noise from within the unit and the locking mechanism clicked back into place.

"Who set this up?"

"I think I might have done," said Johnny, taking the screwdriver back and putting it in his pocket.

"Did you drop it, by any chance?"

"Well, it rolled out of the box when I opened it, but I was kneeling down and the box was on the ground."

"I've told you all before that if we drop one we are not to use until we've put it through a full safety check."

"Yes, but I didn't actually drop it," said Johnny, "it just rolled out of the box and onto the ground."

"And in doing so," said Eddie, "it got some dirt in it which stopped it from working. It could have resulted in quite a serious accident. At least we know there isn't a general fault with them, and it looks as though this one is working again, although I want it fully checked and tested before we use it again.

"Remember," he added, as he put the Auto Belay away, "safety first, ladies and gentlemen, safety first."

* * * * *

The girls were standing in their Sixes in a circle in front of Brown Owl.

"Have we all had a good time?" she said, looking around the circle of twenty-four girls, standing quietly in their Sixes and looking back at her.

"Yes, thank you," the girls all replied together, once again cheering and jumping about. Brown Owl was always very strict that the girls of her Brownie Pack said 'please' and 'thank you'. "Good manners cost nothing and mean everything," she always said and she often thought that, if good manners were the only thing that her girls learned from being one of her Brownies, then it was a lesson well learned.

"Excellent," she continued, "well a number of you have earned some Brownie Badges this weekend, and I will award them to you on our first meeting at the start of the new term. Now, I can see a number of mums and dads waiting to take you home, but before you go, can I remind you not to leave without letting your assigned Pack Leader know. Once again, girls, please show your appreciation for Tawny Owl, Snowy Owl, and Barn Owl, all of whom have worked so hard this weekend for your enjoyment."

"And Brown Owl," someone else shouted out as all the girls once again clapped and cheered.

"One more thing," said Brown Owl as the noise once again died down, "thank you all and well done for making your Pack Holiday such a wonderful weekend, and we all hope you enjoy the final few weeks of your summer holidays and we look forward to seeing you all at Brownies in the new term."

As the girls turned to run off and meet with their parents, Brown Owl called Becca over to her.

"I'll need to speak to your mummy," she said, "about what happened at the end of the Crate Stack Challenge."

"My Mummy won't be here, Brown Owl," she replied, worried that Brown Owl might make her stay and wait until Mummy came instead, "I'm going home with Emma."

"Ah, yes, of course. I'd completely forgotten. I'll have to call her then. Perhaps I can have a quick word with Emma's mummy before you all go."

The field was clearing as the Brownies were collected by their mums and dads and they signed out with the Pack Leaders. Becca looked up and saw Patch, Emma's dog, bounding across the field with Emma.

"Patch!" she called and Patch, with a friendly bark of recognition, bounded over to her and jumped up to lick her face.

"Stop it, you old softie," Becca laughed, throwing her arms around Patch's neck and giving him a warm, friendly, cuddle.

Patch wriggled in her arms and wagged his tail furiously. He had missed the girls.

He gave Becca's face another big wet lick then he ran back to Emma. Then he was charging in a circle around the two girls, barking frantically, as they walked back to the camp pavilion.

Brown Owl was talking to Emma's Mummy as they crossed the car park towards the car.

Patch sat down, panting and looked up expectantly as Emma opened the back door of Mummy's car, put a bowl down in front of him, and filled it with water from a bottle.

As Patch drank noisily from his bowl, splashing as much water as he drank, Becca looked around her; at the trees; at the fields; the pavilion; and the paths that led around the campsite.

She sighed happily. It had been a wonderful weekend.

"I do hope Lily and Cornflower are alright," she said to Emma as they got into the car.

* * * * *

Fairies can fly fast. Very fast. So fast, in fact, that they are capable of overtaking a bullet fired from a gun.

They also have very good hearing. They can hear a worm coughing when it is ten feet under the ground.

When the stack of crates that Becca and Emma were on collapsed they could hear the mechanism of Emma's Auto Belay click into action as it gently lowered her to the ground.

They immediately knew that something was wrong with Becca's Auto Belay as they didn't hear the mechanism click and, faster than a speeding bullet, they flew below her to create an invisible, and magic, cushion of air to slow her fall.

Round and round they flew, faster and faster, they went, singing a flying spell at the top of their voices, as they flew beneath her.

It took a great deal of Fairy Magic for the two tiny Fairies to support a heavy human being, even one as light as Becca, who was only quite small, and it wasn't very long before Lily and Cornflower were exhausted, and Becca was still a long way off the ground.

"We've …. got …. to …. keep …. going," Lily gasped, the two Fairies were calling on their last reserves of energy and their last ounce of Magic. They were desperate to save Becca, but were struggling to keep going.

She and Cornflower sang as loud as they could to maintain the spell that was protecting Becca from falling and hurting herself.

Just as it seemed their Magic was going to fail them there was a flash of red and pink and they were joined by Rose and Petunia who, being fresh, were able to take some of the Magical burden from the two exhausted Fairies.

Slowly, but surely, they lowered Becca safely to the ground.

As Becca was lowered into the hands of the instructors, and quickly passed to Brown Owl, Lily and Cornflower fell, exhausted and unconscious, towards the ground.

Immediately there were streaks of colour from all around the campsite as they were caught and taken in the arms of other Fairies and carried away into the woods, where they would be allowed to recover.

* * * * *

And so the Brownie Pack Holiday weekend came to an end.

The children had had a great deal of fun, and there was so much to tell their Mummies and Daddies when they got home; the fun of the treasure hunt on Saturday afternoon, after they had helped to prepare the food for their evening meal; the rescue of the baby hedgehog before they lit the campfire, after having eaten their fill of burgers that the Pack Leaders had cooked for them; the campfire songs and games which had had them falling down with laughter, followed by the excitement of the twilight nature trail.

"Gosh," Mummy said, laughing, as Becca stopped to take a breath, speaking really fast in her excitement, "what a fun packed day that was. I bet you slept ever so well after that."

"Well …" Becca started, and was just about to tell Mummy about the Unicorn, when she stopped herself. "Yes, we had some hot chocolate and went straight to sleep."

Mummy smiled. She knew Becca was not telling her the whole truth. She knew that Becca and her friends had, almost certainly, talked late into the night, probably falling asleep in the early hours of the following morning. Oh yes, Mummy knew Becca hadn't fallen straight to sleep, she'd been a Brownie herself when she was Becca's age.

"I spoke with Brown Owl earlier," Mummy said, "she told me about what happened at the end of the Crate Stack Challenge."

"I was alright, Mummy," Becca said, "I promise."

"I can see that, because you're here with me now and you've told me all about how wonderful your weekend was. Were you frightened?"

"I was a bit," she replied.

"Just a bit?"

"Well, quite a bit," Becca said, "but everyone was really good, and I was alright in the end."

Happy and assured that Becca wasn't going to have nightmares from her experience, Mummy hugged her brave daughter and then changed the subject.

"Dinner will be ready in a minute, so go and wash your hands, young lady, and after dinner you can unpack your things. I'm sure you've brought home plenty of washing."

"Can I go out to play after dinner?"

"Only when you've unpacked."

* * * * *

The sun continued to shine for the rest of the summer holiday.

It would only be a couple more weeks and then they'd all be going back to school. Both Becca's and Emma's Mummies had been into town and already bought new school uniforms for each of their children.

"They grow so quickly," said Becca's Mummy when she was out uniform shopping with Emma's Mummy.

"And new clothes are just so expensive."

"It's the shoes," replied Becca's Mummy, "Becca grows out of her shoes every few months, and Liam never keeps a pair of shoes long enough to grow out of them, he always manages to ruin them within a few weeks."

Emma's Mummy laughed, "My two are the same," she said, "I've only got to dress Robbie in something brand new and by the time he gets downstairs it looks scruffy on him."

For Becca and Emma that was something to worry about another day, they just wanted to make the most of what was left of the holidays before going back to school.

A few days after the Pack Holiday had finished Becca and Emma were delighted, and excited, to see Lily and Cornflower flying about in the garden, waiting for the two girls to come out and play with them in their enchanted forest.

The End

Printed in Great Britain
by Amazon